AMERICAN HUMORISTS SERIES

OLD ABE'S JOKES

LITERATURE HOUSE / GREGG PRESS
Upper Saddle River, N. J.

Republished in 1969 by
LITERATURE HOUSE
an imprint of The Gregg Press
121 Pleasant Avenue
Upper Saddle River, N. J. 07458

Standard Book Number—8398-1450-X
Library of Congress Card—77-91089

77593

Printed in United States of America

THE AMERICAN HUMORISTS

Art Buchwald, Bob Hope, Red Skelton, S. J. Perelman, and their like may serve as reminders that the "cheerful irreverence" which W. D. Howells, two generations ago, noted as a dominant characteristic of the American people has not been smothered in the passage of time. In 1960 a prominent Russian literary journal called our comic books "an infectious disease." Both in Russia and at home, Mark Twain is still the best-loved American writer; and Mickey Mouse continues to be adored in areas as remote as the hinterland of Taiwan. But there was a time when the mirthmakers of the United States were a more important element in the gross national product of entertainment than they are to-day. In 1888, the British critic Grant Allen gravely informed the readers of the *Fortnightly*: "Embryo Mark Twains grow in Illinois on every bush, and the raw material of *Innocents Abroad* resounds nightly, like the voice of the derringer, through every saloon in Iowa and Montana." And a half-century earlier the English reviewers of our books of humor had confidently asserted them to be "the one distinctly original product of the American mind"—"an indigenous home growth." Scholars are today in agreement that humor was one of the first vital forces in making American literature an original entity rather than a colonial adjunct of European culture.

The American Humorists Series represents an effort to display both the intrinsic qualities of the national heritage of native prose humor and the course of its development. The books are facsimile reproductions of original editions hard to come by—some of them expensive collector's items. The series includes examples of the early infiltration of the autochthonous into the stream of jocosity and satire inherited from Europe but concentrates on representative products of the outstanding practitioners. Of these the earliest in point of time are the exemplars of the Yankee "Down East" school, which began to flourish in the 1830's—and, later, provided the cartoonist Thomas Nast with the idea for Uncle Sam, the national personality in striped pants. The series follows with the chief humorists who first used the Old Southwest as setting. They were the founders of the so-called frontier humor.

The remarkable burgeoning of the genre during the Civil War period is well illustrated in the books by David R. Locke, "Bill Arp," and others who accompanied Mark Twain on the way to fame in the jesters' bandwagon. There is a volume devoted to Abraham Lincoln as jokesmith and spinner of tall tales. The wits and satirists of the Gilded Age, the Gay Nineties, and the first years of the present century round out the sequence. Included also are several works which mark the rise of Negro humor, the sort that made the minstrel show the first original contribution of the United States to the world's show business.

The value of the series to library collections in the field of American literature is obvious. And since the subjects treated in these books, often with surprising realism, are intimately involved with the political and social scene, and the Civil War, and above all possess sectional characteristics, the series is also of immense value to the historian. Moreover, quite a few of the volumes carry illustrations by the ablest cartoonists of their day, a matter of interest to the student of the graphic arts. And, finally, it should not be overlooked that the specimens of Negro humor offer more tangible evidence of the fixed stereotyping of the Afro-American mentality than do the slave narratives or the abolitionist and sociological treatises.

The American Humorists Series shows clearly that a hundred years ago the jesters had pretty well settled upon the topics that their countrymen were going to laugh at in the future—from the Washington merry-go-round to the pranks of local hillbillies. And as for the tactics of provoking the laugh, these old masters long since have demonstrated the art of titillating the risibilities. There is at times mirth of the highbrow variety in their pages: neat repartee, literary parody, Attic salt, and devastating irony. High seriousness of purpose often underlies their fun, for many of them wrote with the conviction that a column of humor was more effective than a page of editorials in bringing about reform or combating entrenched prejudices. All of the time-honored devices of the lowbrow comedians also abound: not only the sober-faced exaggeration of the tall tale, outrageous punning, and grotesque spelling, but a boisterous Homeric joy in the rough-and-tumble. There may be more beneath the surface, however, for as one of their number, J. K. Bangs, once remarked, these old humorists developed "the exuberance of feeling and a resentment of restraint that have helped to make us the free and independent people that we are." The native humor is indubitably American, for it is infused with the customs, associations, convictions, and tastes of the American people.

PROFESSOR CLARENCE GOHDES
Duke University
Durham, North Carolina

January, 1969

OLD ABE'S JOKES,

FRESH FROM

ABRAHAM'S BOSOM

CONTAINING ALL ITS ISSUES,

EXCEPTING THE "GREENBACKS,"

TO CALL IN SOME OF WHICH,

THIS WORK IS ISSUED.

NEW YORK:
T. R. DAWLEY, PUBLISHER,
13 & 15 PARK ROW.

Old Abe's Jokes, says the *New York Herald*, "are the essence of President's Lincoln's life." They will be read by everybody, containing as they do all the JESTS and SQUIBS of Father Abraham.

NOTICE:—Many of these Jokes, Jests and Squibs, contained in this work, never before appeared in print, being fresh from the National Joker's lips, and are entered according to Act of Congress; hence, parties publishing them without crediting to this work, will be liable to prosecution.

T. R. DAWLEY, Stereotyper, Steam Book, Job and Newspaper Printer and Publisher, No. 13 and 15 Park Row, N. Y.

OLD ABE'S JOKES.

Father Abraham's Boyhood, Pots and Kettles, Dutch Ovens, Frying
Pans, Æsops Fables, Rail-Splitting, &c., &c.

Abraham Lincoln was born in Hardin county, Kentucky,
in the year 1809. His parents were poor, and lived in a
log-house "without a floor, furnished with four or five three-
legged stools, pots, kettles, a spider, Dutch oven, and something that answered for a bed." They were both members
of the Baptist church, the mother being represented as a
whole-hearted Christian of godly example and precept.
She could read but could not write. The father was not
so highly endowed by nature as his wife, but was superior
in most respects to his neighbors. He could write his name
but could not read at all.

Abraham was seven years old when he was sent to
school, for the first time, to one Hazel, who came to live in
the neighborhood. There were no schools nor school-houses

in the region, and few of the people could read. But this Hazel could read and write; but beyond this he made a poor figure. For a small sum he taught a few children at his house, and Abraham was one of the number. His parents were so anxious that he should know how to read and write, that they managed to save enough out of their penury to send him to school a few weeks. They considered Abraham a remarkable boy.

Every day he posted away with the old spelling-book to Hazel's cabin, where he tried as hard to learn as any boy who ever studied his Ab's. He carried his book home at night and puzzled his active brain over what he had learned during the day. He cared for nothing but his book. His highest ambition was to learn to read as well as his mother could. As she gathered the family, and read the bible to them each day, and particularly as she read it upon the Sabbath much of the time, he almost envied her the blessed privilege of reading. He longed for the day to come when he could read aloud from that revered volume. Beyond that privilege he did not look. To be able to read was boon enough for him, without looking for anything beyond.

Young Abraham received the most excellent moral teachings from his mother who was accustomed to read the Bible gularly to her family.

Her reading was not confined to the Old Testament, nor to the narrative portions of the Bible. She understood the gospel because she had a Christian experience that was marked. She was a firm, consistent disciple of the Lord Jesus, and was qualified thereby to expound the scriptures. The story of the Cross, as it is recorded in the 27th chapter of Matthew, was read over at the fire-side, accompanied with many remarks that were suited to impress the minds of her children.

The Ten Commandments were made an important matter in the Sabbath lessons, and Abraham was drilled in repeating them, were pressed upon his attention namely, (III) 'Thou shalt not take name of the Lord thy God in vain; for the Lord will not hold him guiltless that taketh his name in vain. (IV.) Remember the Sabbath day to keep it holy.' (V.) 'Honor thy father and thy mother, that thy days may be long upon the land which the Lord hath giveth thee.' (IX.) 'Thou shalt not bear false witness against thy neighbor.'

'In this way many Sabbaths of Abraham's boyhood were spent, so that he became familiar with the Bible. For a boy of his age, he was excelled by few in his acquaintance with the Scriptures. The Bible, catechism, and the old spelling-book named, being the only books in the family at this time, as we have said, and there being no papers, either religious or secular, the Bible was read much more than it would have been if other volumes had been possessed. It was the first book that Abraham ever read—that same old family Bible, kept very choice because their poverty could not afford another. It was the only bible that his mother ever possessed, her life treasure, to which she was more indebted, and perhaps, also, her son Abraham, than any other influence. It was certainly the light of her dwelling, and the most powerful educator that ever entered her family.

That same Bible is still in the possession of a relative in the state of Illinois.

When Abraham was about eight years old, his father, preferring to live in a free State, sold his farm for a lot of whiskey (most of which he lost in moving), and emigrated te Spencer county, Indiana. Here, miles from any neighbor, he opened his new settlement and built himself a cabin, almost the counterpart of the one they had left in Kentucky. About the end of their first year's residence in Indiana, affliction came upon the household in the shape of the death of Mrs. Lincoln. About this time, too, Abraham's literary treasures were enlarged by the acquisition of the *Pilgrim's Progress and Æsop's Fables.*

He read it over and over until he could repeat almost the entire contents of the volume. He was interested in the moral lesson that each fable taught, and derived therefrom many valuable hints that he carried with him through life. On the whole he spent more time over *Æsop's Fables* than he did over *Pilgrim's Progress,* although he was really charmed by the latter. But there was a practical turn to the *Fables* that interested him, and he could easily recollect the stories. Perhaps this early familiarity with this book laid the foundations for that facility at apt story-telling which has distinguished him from his youth. It is easy to see how such a volume might beget and foster a taste in this direction.

He was also so fortunate as to find a writing-master.

Abraham was awkward enough in the use of the pen at first ; but he soon overcame this difficulty, and exhibited unusual judgment for a boy in the formation of letters.— When he had learned how to form a letter, he practiced upon it in various ways. With a bit of chalk he would cut them on pieces of slabs and on the trunks of trees; and

more than once the tops of the stools in the cabin and the
puncheon-table served him in lieu of a writing-book. His
father was too poor to provide him with all the paper necessary for his scribbling, and so he resorted to these various expedients. The end of a charred stick was used as
a pencil sometimes to accomplish his object, and it enabled
him to cut letters with considerable facility.

We have not space to follow Abraham during the course
of his life in Indiana. We pass on to the removal of the
family to Illinois and to the celebrated splitting of the
rails.

They accomplished the journey from Spencer county, Indiana, to Decatur, Illinois, in fifteen days. The spot selected for their home was on the north side of the Sanga-
mon River, about 10 miles west of Decatur, a spot wisely
chosen, because it was at the junction of the timber and
prairie lands.

A log house was immediately erected, in the building of
which Abraham acted a conspicuous part. Ten acres of
prairie land were selected, and the sods were broken for a
crop of corn.

'That must be fenced at once,' said Abraham.

'And you'll have to split the rails, if it is done,' replied
his father.

'That I can do, as I am used to it; but I don't expect to
split rails for a living all my days.'

'I hope you won't have to. When we get things under
way, you can seek your fortin' somewhere else.'

'I haven't made up my mind as to that. There will be
time enough for that when the ten acres are fenced in.'

'We shall have enough to do this summer to break up

and plant ten acres of corn, and take care of it, and fence the lot. But who ever saw such land as this ? The half was not told us.' Mr. Lincoln was surprised at the richness of the lands ; and, in all respects, he was pleased with the change of residence.

'There can be no better farming land than this,' answered Abraham, ' and it ain't half the work to cultivate these prairie lands. And I am just the hand to fence them, as I have swung the axes so much.'

' Yes, you can do it better than I can, and a great deal quicker ; so you may go at it as soon as you please.'

Accordingly, Abraham proceeded to split the rails for the ten acre lot. These are the rails about which so much was said in the late Presidential campaign. ' Their existence,' says Mr. Scripps, ' was brought to the public attention during the sitting of the Republican State Convention, at Decatur, on which occasion a banner, attached to two of these rails, and bearing an appropriate inscription was brought into the assemblage and formally presented to that body, amid a scene of unparalleled enthusiasm. After that they were in demand in every State of the Union in which free labor is honored, where they were borne in processions of the people, and hailed by hundreds of thousands of freemen, as a symbol of triumph, and as a glorious vindication of freedom, and of the rights and the dignity of free labor. These, however, were far from being the first or only rails made by Lincoln. He was a practiced hand at the business. His first lessons were taken while yet a boy in Indiana. Some of the rails made by him in that State have been clearly identified. The writer has seen a cane, now in the possession of Mr. Lincoln, made by one of his old acquaintances, from one of those rails split by his own hands in boyhood.'

Shortly after the removal to Illinois, Abraham left his home to look out for himself. He found a comfortable place with a family living near Petersburg, Menard county, where, as was the case wherever he lived, he acquired the esteem of all.

The young people who became acquainted with him gave him their confidence without hesitation. They believed him to be a conscientious, upright young man. For this reason, they referred the settlement of dispute to him. They had confidence in his judgment as well as his honesty. Different sorts of games were in vogue at that time, and running matches and horse-racings, and if Abraham was present, one party or the other was sure to make him their judge. Two years later, while he was living in New Salem, he shared the confidence of all to such an extent that *both* parties, in the aforesaid amusements, were wont to choose him for their judge. In all cases. too, there was the utmost satisfaction shown in his decisions.

It was at this period of his life that he was christened ' Honest Abe.' It was so unusual for the same person to act as judge for both of the contending parties, and it was expressive of so much confidence in his character that by common consent he came to be known as ' HONEST ABE.'

———o———

Father Abraham a Disciple of "Father Matthew."

When Gen. Hooker was ordered to join Gen. Grant at Chattanooga, the president advised him to avoid *'Bourbon'* county, when passing through Kentucky.

An Englishman's Portraits of Old Abe

' To say that he is ugly, is nothing; to add that his figure is grotesque, is to convey no adequate impression.—
Fancy a man six feet high, and then out of proportion;
with long bony arms and legs, which somehow seem to be
always in the way; with great rugged furrowed hands,
which grasp you like a vice when shaking yours; with a
long snaggy neck, and a chest too narrow for the great
arms at its side. Add to this figure a head cocoa-nut
shaped and somewhat too small for such a stature, covered
with rough, uncombed and uncomable hair, that stands out
in every direction at once; a face furrowed, wrinkled and
indented, as though it had been scarred by vitrol; a high
narrow forehead; and sunk deep beneath bushy eyebrows,
two bright, dreamy eyes, that seem to gaze through you
without looking at you; a few irregular blotches of black
bristly hair, in the place where beard and whiskers ought
to grow; a close-set, thin-lipped, stern mouth, with two
rows of large white teeth, and a nose and ears which have
been taken by mistake from a head of twice the size.—
Clothe this figure, then, in a long, tight, badly-fitting suit
of black, creased, soiled and puckered up at every salient
point of the figure (and every point of this figure is salient)
put on large, ill-fitting boots, gloves too long for the long
bony fingers, and a fluffy hat, covered to the top with
dusty, puffy crape; and then add to this an air of strength,
physical as well as moral, and a strange look of dignity
coupled with all this grotesqueness; and you will have the
impression left upon me by Abraham Lincoln.'

An American's Portrait of Father Abraham.

In character and culture he is a fair representative of the average American. His awkward speech and yet more awkward silence, his uncouth manners, self-taught and partly forgotten, his style miscellaneous, concreted from the best authors, like a reading book, and yet oftentimes of Saxon force and classic purity ; his argument, his logic a joke ; both unseasonable at times and irresistable always ; his questions answers, and his answers questions ; his guesses prophecies, and fulfillment ever beyond his promise ; honest yet shrewd ; simple yet retiscent ; heavy yet energetic ; never despairing, never sanguine ; careless in forms, conscientious in essentials ; never sacrificing a good servant once trusted ; never deserting a good principle once adopted ; not afraid of new ideas, nor despising old ones ; improving opportunities to confess mistakes, ready to learn, getting at facts, doing nothing when he knows not what to do ; hesitating at nothing when he sees the right ; lacking the recognized qualifications of a party leader, and leading his party as no other man can ; sustaining his political enemies in Missouri in their defeat, sustaining his political friends in Maryland to their victory ; conservative in his sympathies and radical in his acts, Socratic in his style and Baconian in his method ; his religion consisting in truthfulness, temperance : asking good people to pray for him, and publicly acknowledging in events the hand of God, yet he stands before you as the type of ' Brother Jonathan,' a not perfect man and yet more precious than fine gold.'

The President in Society.

'On the occasion when the writer had the honor of meeting the President, the company was a small one, with most of whom he was personally acquainted. He was much at his ease. There was a look of depression about his face, which was habitual to him even before his child's death. It was strange to me to witness the perfect terms of equality on which he appeared to be with everybody. Occasionally some of his interlocutors called to him: 'Mr. President,' but the habit was to address him simply as: 'Sir.' It was not, indeed, till we were introduced to him that we were aware that the President was one of the company. He talked little, and seemed to prefer others talking to him to talking himself; but, when he spoke, his remarks were always shrewd and sensible. You would never say he was a gentleman; you would still less say he was not one. There are some women about whom no one ever thinks in connection with beauty one way or the other; and there are men to whom the epithet of gentleman-like or ungentleman-like appears utterly incongruous; and of such Mr. Lincoln is one. Still there is about him an utter absence of pretension, and an evident desire to be courteous to everybody, which is the essence, if not the outward form, of good breeding. There is a softness, too, about his smile, and a sparkle of dry humor about his eye, which redeem the expression of his face, and remind us more of the late Dr. Arnold, as a child's recollection recalls him, than of any face we can call to mind.

The conversation, like that of all American official men

we have met with, was unrestrained in the presence of strangers, to a degree perfectly astonishing. Any remarks that we heard made, as to the present state of affiairs, we do not feel at liberty to repeat, though really every public man here appears not only to live in a glass house, but in a reverberating gallery, and to be absolutely indifferent as to who sees or hears him. Tnere are a few ' Lincolnisms,' however, which we may fairly quote, and which will show the style of his conversation. Some of the party began smoking, and our host remarked, laughingly, ' The President has got no vices: he neither smokes nor drinks.' 'That is a doubtful compliment,' answered the President ' I recollect once being outside a stage in Illinois, and a man sitting by me offered me a cigar. I told him I had no vices. He said nothing, smoked for some time, and then grunted out, ' its my experience that folks who have no vices have plaguy few virtues.' Again a gentleman present was telling how a friend of his had been driven away from New Orleans as a Unionist, and how, on his expulsion, when he asked to see the writ by which he was expelled, the deputation which called on him told him that the Government had made up their minds to do nothing illegal, and so they had issued no illegal writs, and simply meant to *make* him go of his own free will. ' Well,' said Mr. Lincoln, ' that reminds me of a hotel keeper down at St. Louis, who boasted he never had a death in his hotel, for whenever a guest was dying in his house he carried him out to die in the street.'

Mr. Lincoln's Daily Life.

' Mr. Lincoln is an early riser, and he thus is able to devote two or three hours each morning to his voluminous
private correspondence, besides glancing at a city paper.
At nine he breakfasts—then walks over to the war office,
to read such war telegrams as they give him, (occasionally
some are withheld,) and to have a chat with General Halleck on the military situation, in which he takes a great interest.   Returning to the white house, he goes through
with his morning's mail, in company with a private secretary, who makes a minute of the reply which he is to make
—and others the President retains, that he may answer
them himself.   Every letter receives attention, and all
which are entitled to a reply receive one no matter how
they are worded, or how inelegant the chirography may be.
Tuesday and Fridays are cabinet days, but on other
days visitors at the white house are requested to wait in
the anti-chamber, and send in their cards.   Sometimes,
before the President has finished reading his mail Louis
will have a handful of pasteboard, and from the cards laid
before him Mr. Lincoln has visitors ushered in, giving pre-
cedence to acquaintances.   Three or four hours do they
pour in, in rapid succession, nine out of ten asking offices,
and patiently does the president listen to their application.
Care and anxiety have furrowed his rather homely features,
yet occasionally he is 'reminded of an anecdote' and good
humored glances beam from his clear, grey eyes, while his
ringing laugh shows that he is not 'used up' yet.   The

simple and natural manner in which he delivers his
thoughts makes him appear to those visiting him like an
earnest, affectionate friend. He makes little parade of
his legal science, and rarely indulges in speculative propo-
sitions, but states his ideas in plain Angle-saxon, illumina-
ted by many lively images and pleasing allusions, which
seem to flow as if in obedience to a resistless impulse of
his nature. Some newspaper admirer attempts to deny
that the President tells stories. Why, it is rarely that any
one is in his company for fifteen minutes without hearing a
good tale, appropriate to the subject talked about. Many
a metaphysical argument does he demolish by simply telling
an anecdote, which exactly overturns the verbal structure.

About four o'clock the President declines seeing any
more company, and often accompanies his wife in her carriage to take a drive. He is fond of horseback exercise,
and when passing the summers' home used generally to go
in the saddle. The President dines at six, and it is rare
that some personal friends do not grace the round dining
table where he throws off the cares of office, and reminds
those who have been in Kentucky of the old school gentleman who used to dispense generous hospitality there.—
From the dinner table the party retire to the crimson drawing room, where coffee is served, and where the President
passes the evening, unless some dignitary has a special interview. Such is the almost unvarying daily life of Abraham Lincoln, whose administration will rank next in importance to that of Washington in our national annals.'

Personal Habits of the President,

Those who know the habits of President Lincoln are not surprised to hear of his personal visit to some general, nor would any such be astonished to know that he was in New York at any time. If he wanted to see anything or anybody, he would be as likely to come on as to send. He has an orbit of his own, and no one can tell where he will be or what he will do, from anything done yesterday. If he wants a newspaper he is quite as likely to go out and get it as he is to send after it. If he want's to see the Secretary of State, he generally goes out and makes a call. retary of State, he generally goes out and makes a call.— At night, from ten to twelve, he usually makes a tour all around—now at Seward's and then at Halleck's ; and if Burnside was nearer, he would see him each night before he went to bed. Those who know his habits and want to see him late at night, follow him round from place to place, and the last search generally brings him up at Gen. Halleck's, as he can get the latest army intelligence there.— Whoever else is asleep or indolent the President is wide awake and around.

Beneath all the playfulness of his mind burns a solemn earnestness of patriotism; amid his prudence a great courage ; in all his gentleness and compliance a determined grasp of the reins, and a firmness not inferior to General Jackson's, though without its passion and caprice. He is a wise, true, sagacious, earnest and formidable leader.'

Several Little Stories,

BY AND ABOUT PRESIDENT LINCOLN.

'It would be hardly necessary to inform the nation that our President, in the midst of the anxieties of a state of war that continually torture his mind, is wont to find occasional relief in an appropriate anecdote or well-turned jest.

No man, says Mrs. Stowe, has suffered more and deeper, albeit with a dry, weary, patient pain, that seemed to some like insensibility, than President Lincoln. 'Whichever way it ends,' he said to the writer, 'I have the impression that *I* shan't last much longer after it is over.'

After the dreadful repulse of Fredericksburg, he is reported to have said : 'If there is a man out of Hell that suffers more than I do, I pity him.' In those dark days his heavy eyes and worn and weary air told how our reverses wore upon him, and yet there was a never-failing fund of patience at the bottom, that sometimes rose to the surface in some droll, quaint saying or story, that forced a laugh even from himself.

————o————

Old Abe Consulting the Spirits.

A Washington correspondent of the Boston *Saturday Evening Gazette*, gives the following account of a *spiritual* manifestation at the White House :

'A few evenings since Abraham Lincoln, the President of the United States, was induced to give a Spiritual soiree in the crimson room at the White House, to test the won-

derful alleged supernatural powers of Mr. Charles E.
Shockle. It was my good fortune as a friend of the medium to be present, the party consisting of the President,
Mrs. Lincoln, Mr. Welles, Mr. Stanton, Mr. L., of New
York, and Mr. F., of Philadelphia. We took our seats in
the circle about eight o'clock, but the President was called
away shortly after the manifestations commenced, and the
spirits, which had apparently assembled to convince him of
their power, gave visible tokens of their displeasure at
the President's absence, by pinching Mr. Stanton's ears
and twitching Mr. Welles' beard. The President soon returned, but it was some time before harmony was restored,
for the mishaps to the Secretaries caused such bursts of
laughter, that the influence was very unpropitious. For
some half hour the demonstrations were of a physical character—tables were moved, and a picture of Henry Clay,
which hangs on the wall, was swayed more than a foot, and
two candelabras, presented by the Dey of Algiers to President Adams, were twice raised nearly to the ceiling.

It was nearly nine o'clock before Shockle was fully under
spiritual influence, and so powerful were the subsequent
manifestations that twice during the evening restoratives
were applied, for he was much weakened, and though I
took no notes, I shall endeavor to give you as faithful an
account as possible of what took place.

Loud rappings about nine o'clock were heard directly
beneath the President's feet, and Mr. Shockle stated that
an Indian desired to communicate.

'Well, sir,' said the President, 'I should be happy to
hear what his Indian majesty has to say. We have recently had a visitation from our red brethren, and it was the

only delegation, black, white or blue, which did not volunteer some advice about the conduct of the war.'

The medium then called for pencil and paper, and they were laid upon the table in sight of all. A handkerchief was then taken from Mr. Stanton, and the materials were carefully concealed from sight. In less space of time than it has required me to write this, knocks were heard, and the paper was uncovered. To the surprise of all present, it read as follows:

"Haste makes waste, but delays cause vexations. Give vitality by energy. Use every means to subdue. Proclamations are useless. Make a bold front and fight the enemy, leave traitors at home to the care of the loyal men. Less note of preparation, less parade and policy-talk and more action.   HENRY KNOX."

'That is not Indian talk, Mr. Shockle,' said the President. 'Who is Henry Knox?'

I suggested to the medium to ask who General Knox was, and before the words were from my lips, the medium spoke in a strange voice, 'The first Secretary of War.'

'Oh, yes, General Knox,' said the President, who turning to the Secretary, said, 'Stanton, that message is for you—it is from your predecessor.'

Mr. Stanton made no reply.

'I should like to ask General Knox,' said the President, 'if it is within the scope of his ability to tell us when this rebellion will be put down.'

In the same manner as before this message was received:

'Washington, Lafayette, Franklin, Wilberforce, Napoleon and myself have held frequent consultations upon this point. There is something which our spiritual eyes cannot detect which prevents rapid consummation of plans which appear well formed. Evil has come at times by removal of men from high positions, and there are those in retirement whose abilities should be made useful to hasten the end. Napoleon says concentrate your forces upon one point, Lafayette thinks that the rebellion will die of exhaustion, Franklin sees the end approaching as the South must give up for want of mechanical ability to compete against Northern mechanics, Wilberforce sees hope only in a negro army.   KNOX.'

'Well,' exclaimed the President, ' opinions differ among the saints as well as among the sinners. They don't seem to understand running the machine among the celestials much better than we do. Their talk and advice sound very much like the talk of my cabinet—don't you think so Mr. Welles?'

'Well, I don't know—I will think the matter over and see what conclusions I arrive at.'

Heavy raps were heard and the alphabet was called for when ' That's what's the matter' was spelled out.

There was a shout of laughter, and Mr. Welles stroked his beard.

'That means, Mr. Welles,' said the President, ' that you are apt to be long-winded, and think the nearest way home is the longest round. Short cuts in war times. I wish the spirits would tell us how to catch the Alabama.'

The lights which had been partially lowered almost instantaneously become so dim that I could not see sufficiently to distinguish the features of any one in the room, and on the large mirror over the mantel-peice there appeared the most beautiful though supernatural picture eye ever beheld. It represented a sea-view, the Alabama with all steam up flying from the pursuit of another large steamer. Two merchantmen in the distance were seen partially destroyed by fire. The picture changed and the Alabama was seen at anchor under the shadow of an English fort—from which an English flag was flying. The Alabama was floating idly, not a soul on board, and no signs of life visible about her.

The picture vanished and in letters of purple appeared, 'The English PEOPLE demand this of England's ARISTOCRACY.'

'So England is to seize the Alabama finally?' said the President. 'It may be possible, but Mr. Welles, don't let one gunboat or one monitor less be built.'

The spirits again called for the alphabet, and again 'That's what's the matter' was spelt out.

'I see, I see,' said the President. 'Mother England thinks that what's sauce for the goose may be sauce for the gander. It may be tit, tat, too hereafter But it is not very complimentary to our Navy anyhow.'

'We've done our best, Mr. President,' said Mr. Welles. 'I'm maturing a plan, which, when perfected, I think if it works well, will be a perfect trap for the Alabama.'

'Well, Mr. Shockle,' remarked the President, 'I have seen strange things and heard rather odd remarks but nothing which convinces me, except the pictures, that there is anything very heavenly about all this. I should like if possible, to hear what Judge Douglas says about this war.'

'I'll try to get his spirit,' said Mr. Shockle, 'but it

sometimes happens, as it did to-night in the case of the Indian, that though first impressed by one spirit, I yield to another more powerful. If perfect silence is maintained, I will see if we cannot induce General Knox to send for Mr. Douglas.'

Three raps were given, signifying assent to the proposition. Perfect silence was maintained, and after an interval of perhaps three minutes, Mr. Shockle rose quickly from his chair and stood behind it, resting his left arm on the back, his right thrust into his bosom. In a voice such as no one could mistake who had ever heard Mr. Douglas, he spoke. I shall not pretend to quote the language. It was eloquent and choice. He urged the President to throw aside all advisers who hesitated about the policy to be pursued, and to listen to the wishes of the people, who would sustain him at all points, if his aim was, as he believed it was, to restore the Union. He said there were Burrs and Blenderhassetts still living, but that they would wither before the popular approval, which would follow one or two victories, such as he thought must take place ere long. The turning point in this war will be the proper use of these victories; if wicked men in the first hours of success think it time to devote their attention to party, the war will be prolonged, but if victory is followed up by energetic action *all will be well.*

'I believe that,' said the President, ' whether it comes from spirit or human.'

Mr. Shockle was much prostrated after this, and at Mrs. Lincoln's request it was thought best to adjourn the seance *sine die.*

" Too Cussed Dirty."

The following story is often told of Father Abraham about two contrabands, servants of General Kelly and Capt. George Harrison. When the General and his staff were on their way up the mountains they stopped at a little village to get something to eat. They persuaded the occupant of the farm-house to cook them a meal, and in order to expedite matters, sent the two contrabands mentioned to assist in preparing the repast. After it was over the General told the negroes to help themselves. An hour or two afterward he observed them gnawing away at some hard crackers and flitch.

' Why didn't you eat your dinner at the village ?' asked the General of one of them.

' Well, to tell the God's trufe, General, it wos too cussed dirty !' was the reply.

————o————

Old Abe on Bayonets.

' You can't do anything with them Southern fellows, the old gentleman at the table was saying. ' If they get whipped they'll retreat to them Southern swamps aud bayous along with the fishes and crocodiles. You haven't got the fish-nets made that'll catch 'em.' 'Look here, old gentleman !' screamed old Abe, who was sitting along side ' We've got just the nets for traitors, in the bayous or anywhere. ' Hey ?—what nets ?' ' *Bayou.nets ?*' and Abraham pointed his joke with a fork, spearing a fishball savagely.

Old Abe as a Mathematician.

Mr. Lincoln has a very effective way sometimes of dealing with men who trouble him with questions. Somebody asked him how many men the rebels had in the field. He replied very seriously, 'Twelve hundred thousand, according to the best authority.' The interrogator blanched in the face, and ejaculated 'My God!' 'Yes, sir, twelve hundred thousand—no doubt of it. You see, all of our Generals, when they get whipped, say the enemy outnumbers them from three or five to one, and I must believe them. We have four hundred thousand men in the field, and three times four make twelve. Don't you see it?' The inquisitive man looked for his hat soon after ' seeing it.'

———o———

Father Abe on the Wooden-legged Amateur.

Old Abe, once reminded of the enormous cost of the war, remarked, ah, yes! that reminds me of a wooden legged amateur who happened to be with a Virginia skirmishing party when a shell burst near him, smashing his artificial limb to bits, and sending a piece of iron through the calf of a soldier near him. The soldier ' grinned and bore it' like a man, while the amateur was loud and emphatic in his lamentation. Being rebuked by the wounded soldier, he replied: ' Oh, yes; its all well enough for you to bear it. Your leg didn't cost you anything, and will heal up; but I paid two hundred dollars for mine!'

Lincoln Teaching the Soldier's How to Surrender arms.

As the members of one of our volunteer companies were being practiced in the musket-drill, a gentleman, who, although not of the corps, was acting as Lieutenant for the day, said: ' I will teach you the manner of surrendering arms, so in case you ever have to do it, you will know how to do it gracefully.' Mr. Lincoln standing near, immediately responded: 'Hold on, Lieutenant; I'll teach them that myself.' He seized a musket from a soldier standing near, and raised it to his shoulder a moment, as if in the act of firing upon an enemy ; then letting it drop from his hand, he imitated the action of a man shot through the heart, staggered heavily forward, and fell upon the piece. He sprang up again in a moment and cried ; ' That's the way to surrender arms!' A tremendous shout broke from the ranks. ' That's the kind we learn—surrender and die at the same time; never mind the grace of it. And the ' grace of it' was discarded.'

———o———

Abe's Curiosity.

Father Abraham says he lately discovered in an old drawer which had not been opened for years, a remarkable silver coin, which had on one side a head with the word ' Liberty' surrounded by thirteen stars, and the date 1860. On the opposite was an eagle with the motto ' E Pluribus Unum,' the words ' United States of America,' and the figures ' 10c !'

Lincoln Agreeably Disappointed.

Mr. Lincoln, as the highest public officer of the nation is necessarily very much bored by all sorts of people calling upon him.

An officer of the Government called one day at the White House, and introduced a clerical friend. 'Mr President,' said he, 'allow me to present to you my friend the Rev. Mr. F. of——. Mr. F. has expressed a desire to see you and have some conversation with you, and I am happy to be the means of introducing him.' The President shook hands with Mr. F., and desiring him to be seated took a seat himself. Then—his countenance having assumed an air of patient waiting—he said: 'I am now ready to hear what you have to say.' 'O, bless you, sir,' said Mr. F., 'I have nothing especially to say, I merely called to pay my respects to you, and, as one of the million, to assure you of my hearty sympathy and support.' 'My dear sir,' said the President, rising promptly—his face showing instant relief, and with both hands grasping that of his visitor, 'I am very glad to see you, indeed. *I thought you had come to preach to me!*'

————o————

Secesh Lady.

A Secesh lady of Alexandria, who was ordered away into Dixie by the Government, destroyed all her furniture and cut down her trees, so that the 'cursed Yankees' should not enjoy them. Lincoln hearing of this, the order was countermanded, and she returned to see in her broken penates, the folly of her conduct.

ONE OF ABE'S LAST.—'I can't say for certain who will be the people's choice for President, but to the best of my belief it will be the successful candidate.'

————o————

The following, although not belonging to Father Abe. is not so bad:

Gen. Hindman's mode of financiering.

Gen. Hindman, had resolved to go into the neighboring State of Arkansas, determined to raise a forced loan of one million dollars from the banks of Memphis, four in number. None of the moneyed inhabitants gave very cheerful accord to the demand. The President of one of them hesitated some time, and finally told the General that he could not accommodate him.

'I must have it,' said the general.

'By what authority do you demand it?' asked the bank president.

'By the authority of the sword,' replied Hindman.

'Of course I cannot resist that,' said the financial man.

'I should think not,' responded the rebel commander.

And so it turned out. The money was taken out of the bank vaults by a party of rebel soldiers detailed by Hindman for that purpose.

————o————

'I feel patriotic,' said an old rowdy. 'What do you mean by feeling patriotic?' inquired the President, who was standing by. 'Why, I feel as if I wanted to kill somebody or steal something.' 'The Tennessee authorities felt the same kind of patriotism on the Fourth of July; and as they didn't like to venture upon killing any body; they stole the trains of the Louisville and Nashville Railroad.

————o————

Old Abe's story of New Jersey.

One terribly stormy night in bleak December, a United States vessel was wrecked off the coast of Jersey, and every soul save one, went down with the doomed craft. This one survivor seized a floating spar and was washed toward the shore, while innumerable kind-hearted tools of the Camden and Amboy railroad clustered on the beach with boats and ropes. Slowly the unhappy mariner drifted to land and as he exhaustedly caught at the rope thrown to him, the kindly natives uttered an encouraging cheer. 'You are saved!' they shouted. 'You are saved, and must show the conductor your ticket!' With the sea still boiling about him, the drowning stranger resisted the efforts to haul him ashore. 'Stop!' said he, in faint tones 'tell me where I am! What country is this?' They answered 'New Jersey.' Scarcely had the name been uttered when the wretched stranger let go the rope, ejaculating, as he did so, 'I guess I'll float a little farther!'

————o————

Swearing a Contraband.

The President often tells the following, which may be considered rich. Company K, of the first Iowa Cavalry, stationed in Tennessee, received into their camp a middle-aged but vigorous contraband. Innumerable questions were being propounded to him, when a corporal advanced observing,—'See here, Dixie, before you can enter the service of the United States you must be sworn.'

'Yes, massa, I do dat,' he replied; when the corporal continued:

'Well then, take hold of the Bible,' holding out a letter envelope, upon which was delineated the Goddess of Liberty, standing on a Suffolk pig, wearing the emblem of our country. The negro grasped the envelope cautiously with his thumb and finger, when the corporal proceeded to administer the oath by saying:

'You do solemnly swear that you will support the Constitution of the United States, and see that there are no grounds floating upon the coffee at all times.'

'Yes, massa, I do dat,' he replied ; 'I allers settle him in de coffee-pot.'

Here he let go the envelope to gesticulate by a downward thrust of his forefinger the direction that would be given to the coffee grounds for the future.

'Never mind how you do it,' shouted the corporal, 'but hold on to the Bible.'

'Lordy massa, I forgot,' said the negro, as he darted forward and grasped the envelope with a firmer clutch, when the corporal continued:

'And you do solemnly swear that you will support the Constitution of all loyal States, and not spit upon the plates when cleaning them, or wipe them with your shirt-sleeves.'

Here a frown lowered upon the brow of the negro, his eyes expanded to their largest dimensions, while his lips protruded with a rounded form as he exclaimed:

'Lordy, mássa, I never do dat. I allers washes him
nice. 'Ole missus mighty 'ticler 'bout dat.'

'Never mind ole missus,' shouted the corporal, as he
resumed : 'and do you solemnly swear that you will put
milk into the coffee every morning, and see that the ham
and eggs are not cooked too much or too little.'

'Yes, I do dat, I'se a good cook.'

'And lastly,' continued the corporal, 'you do solemnly
swear that when this war is over you'll make tracks for
Africa mighty fast.'

'Yes, massa, I do dat. I allers wanted to go to Chee-
cargo

Here the regimental drum beat up for dress parade,
when Tom Benton—that being his name—was declared
duly sworn in and commissioned as chief-cook in Company
K. of the first Iowa Cavalry.

————o————

The Jeff. Davis Confederacy is getting so hard up for
troops, that it has commenced the seizure of tobacco-chew-
ers, in order to secure their 'old soldiers.'

————o————

Lincoln and Col. Weller.

Weller was at Washington settling his accounts as
Minister to Mexico. After their adjustment, he concluded
to pay his respects to Mr. Lincoln, with whom he had
served in Congress. He called at the Presidential mansion, and was courteously received. 'Mr. President,' said
Colonel Weller, 'I have called on you to say that I most
heartily endorse the conservative position you have assumed

and will stand by you as long as you prosecute the war for the preservation of the Union and the Constitution.'— ' Colonel Weller,' said the President, ' I am heartily glad to hear you say this.' ' Yes, Mr. President,' said Weller, ' I desire an appointment to aid in this work.' ' What do you want, Colonel?' asked Abraham. '*I desire to be appointed Commodore in the Navy*,' said Weller. The President repled : ' Colonel, I did not think you had any experience as a sailor.' ' I never had, Mr. President,' said Weller ; ' but, judging from the Brigadier-Generals you have appointed in Ohio, the less experience a man has, the higher position he attains.' Lincoln turned off with a hearty laugh, and said : ' I owe you one, Colonel !'

————o————

Mrs. Lincoln's Bonnet.

' Burleigh,' ' gets off ' the following gossip about a bonnet for Mrs. Lincoln :

About the same number of cities that contended—

"For Homer dead,
Through which the living Homer begged his bread."

are contending for the honor of furnishing a hat for the head that reclines on Abraham's bosom. In New York, from Canal street to Fourteenth, from Philadelphia to Bangor, can be seen on exhibition a ' Bonnet for Mrs. President Lincoln.' These establishments send on and notify Mrs. L. that they have a love of a bonnet, which they are desirous to present to her as a testimonial of their loyalty and great regard for her personally. The amiable and kind-hearted lady of the White House (for such she is) condescends to accept the gift, and at once ' Mrs. Lincoln's

Hat,' is on exhibition, and crowds flock to see it.   And
such a hat! a condensed milliner's stock in trade, arched
high enough to admit a canal boat under it, scalloped,
fluted and plaited, loaded with bugles, birds of Paradise,
French lace and gewgaws known by name only to the
trade, black and white crape, with a mingling of ribbons
of all hues, and as many contradictions as there are in a
glass of punch.   A fit capstone to the cranium of a 'Madge
Wildfire.'   Mrs. Lincoln may wear all these bonnets, but
judging from the specimen I saw, 'uneasy lies the head that
wears '—such a bonnet.

————o————

Honest Abe's Replies.

Old Abe being asked what he had done for his country,
made the following reply :

1st. I confiscated their cotton, but in return gave them
' Wool.'

2d. I have exercised a   Foster-ing' care over North
Carolina.

3d. I gave them a 'Pope' to control their misguided
zeal.

4th. Notwithstanding the financial condition of their
country, I established 'Banks' in New Orleans.

5th. I furnished them with a 'Butler' and 'Porter.'

6th. When the slaves in South Carolina fled from their
masters, I sent them a Hunter,' who found them by hundreds.

7th. When they invaded Pennsylvania to reap a har-
vest, I furnished the 'Sickles' and gave them 'Meade' to
cool their heated blood.

The Presidential Hymn of Thanks.

Miles O'Rielly, the soldier who was arrested on Morris Island, S. C., for making poetry, and pardoned by the President, in response to a witty poetical petition, has sent a hymn of thanks to the President, beginning :

" Long life to you, Misther Lincoln ;
   May you die both late and aisy ;
An' whin you lie wid the top of aich toe
   Turned up to the roots of a daisy,
May this be your epitaph, nately writ :
     Though thraitors abused him vilely,
He was honest an' kindly, he loved a joke,
   An' he pardoned Myles O'Rielly.' "

————o————

What Old Abe says of Tennessee.

It is a fertile country, and the people are putting in crops after a fashion, and under difficulties. He asked a lady from there not long ago,

' Will you make a crop of cotton this year ?'

' I am going to try.'

' How many hands have you got ?'

' One woman.'

It struck me, says Abe, that a crop of cotton 'made' by one female citizen of African descent would not be what is generally nominated a 'BIG THING.

A Patriotio (?) Darkey.

Our President also tells the following story:

Upon the hurricane deck of one of our gunboats, an elderly darkey, with a very philosophical and retrospective cast of countenance, squatted upon his bundle, toasting his shins against the chimney and apparently plunged into a state of profound meditation. Finding upon inquiry that he belonged to the Ninth Illinois, one of the most gallantly behaved and heavy losing regiments at the Fort Donelson battle, and part of which was aboard, began to interrogate him upon the subject:

'Were you in the fight?'

'Had a little taste of it' sa.'

'Stood your ground, did you?'

'No, sa, I runs.'

'Run at the first fire, did you?'

'Yes, sa, and would hab run soona, had I knowd it war comin.'

'Why, that wasn't very creditable to your courage.'

'Dat isn't my line, sa—cookin's my profeshun.'

'Well, but have you no regard for your reputation?'

'Reputation's nuffin to me by de side ob life.'

'Do you consider your life worth more than other people's?'

'It's worth more to me, sa.'

'Then you must value it very highly?'

'Yes, sa, I does, more dan all dis wuld, more dan a millian ob dollars sa, for what would dat be wuth to a man wid de bref out obhim? Self-preserbation am de fust law wid me.'

' But why should you act upon a different rule from other men ?'

'Because different men set different values upon their lives; mine is not in de market.'

" But if you lost it, you would have the satisfaction of knowing that you died for your country.'

' What satifaction would dat be to to me when de power of feelin' was gone?'

'Then patriotism and honor are nothing to you ?'

' Nufin whatever, sa—I regard them as among the vani ties.'

' If our soldiers were like you, traitors might have broken up the government without resistance.'

' Yes, sa, dar would hab been no help for it. I wouldnt put my life in de scale 'ginst any gobernment dat eber existed, for no gobernment could replace de loss to me.'

' Do you think any of your company would have missed you if you had been killed ?'

' Maybe not, sa—a dead white man ain't much to dese sogers, let alone a dead nigga—but I'd a missed myself and dat was de pint wid me.'

————o————

Old Abe a Coward.

If Lincoln should be renominated for the Presidency, why would he be a cowardly antagonist? Because he would be sure to run.

Abraham Advise sthe " Springs."

It is stated that Old Abe being much disgusted at the crowd of officers who some time ago used to loiter about the Washington hotels, and he is reported to have remarked to a member of Congress : " These fellows *and the Congressmen* do vex me sorely, they should certainly visit the ' Springs.'

---o---

Lincoln 'Metalic Ring.'

The new fractional notes have upon the face a faint oval ring of bronze encircling the vignette. Upon being asked its use, Mr. Lincoln said: ' It was a faint attempt on the part of Mr. Chase to give the currency a metalic ring.'

---o---

Abe tells the following story about a drunken captain who met a private of his company in the same condition. The captain ordered him to ' halt,' and endeavoring in vain to assume a firm position on his feet, and to talk with dignified severity, exclaimed : ' Private Smith, I'll give you t'l)hic) four o'clock to gissober in." ' Cap'n,' replied the soldier, ' as you'r (hic) —— sight drunkerniam, I'll give you t'l five o'clock to gissober in.'

---o---

Old Abe tells the following anecdote of a prisoner, a Union soldier, a droll-looking fellow. I accosted him with, ' Well, my fine fellow, what are you in here for ?'

' For taking something,' he replied. 'What do you mean?'
' Why,' said he, ' one morning I did not feel very well, and
went to see the surgeon. He was busy writing at the
time, and when I went in he looked at me, saying, ' Well,
you do look bad ; you had better take something,' He
then went on with his writing, and left me standing behind him. I looked around, and saw nothing I could take
except his watch, and I took that. That's what I am in
here for.'

----o----

A Good Word for Mr. Lincoln.

It is some amends for the ridicule which has been un-
sparingly heaped by certain presses upon Mr. Lincoln,
that the *London Spectator*, one of the most intelligent and
most respectable journals in Europe, finds occasion for the
following words about him :

' Mr. Lincoln has been treated, as few governors have
ever been treated, and although he may not always have
risen fully to the level of a great emergency, he has sel-
dom failed to display a noble impartiality, a great firmness of purpose, and a sagacious, if somewhat utilitarian
judgment. We believe a juster man never held the reins
of government.'

----o----

Sinecure vs Water-cure.

' The private secretary of the President is a wag. A
young man decidedly inebriated, walked into the executive mansion and asked for the President,

'What do you want with him?' inquired the Secretary.

'Oh, I want an office with a good salary—a sinecure.'

'Well,' replied the Secretary, • I can tell you something better for you than a sinecure—you had better try *water cure.*'

A new idea seemed to strike the young inebriate and he vamosed.

—————o————

The Negro in a Hogshead.

Abe often laughs over the following:

A curious incident, which escaped general attention at the time of its occurrence, happened at police headquarters during the riot.　While President Acton was giving some final orders to a squad of men who were just leaving to combat the crowd in First avenue, a wagon containing a hogshead was driven rapidly up to the Mulberry street door, by a lad who appeared much excited and almost breathless.

'What have you there, my lad?' said the President.

'Supplies for your men,' was the answer.

'What are they?

'It is an assorted lot, sir ; but the people says it's contraband.'

Being exceedingly busy, the President ordered the wagon to be driven round to the Mott street entrance, where an officer was sent to look after the goods.　When the wagon arrived the officers were about to tip the cask out, but where prevented by the boy, who exclaimed:

'Wait a minute, bring me a hatchet,'　A hatchet was

brought, and the little fellow set to work unheading the cask, and as he did so the officers were astonished to see two full grown negroes snugly packed inside. Upon being assured by the lad that they were safe they raised their heads, took a long snuff of fresh air, and exclaimed, 'Bress de Lord!'

The boy stated that the rioters had chased the poor unfortunates into the rear of some houses on the west side of the town, and that they had escaped by scaling a fence and landing in a grocer's yard; that the grocer was friendly to them, but feared his place might be sacked if they were found there. He accordingly hit upon this novel plan of getting them out, and while he kept watch in front the boy coopered the negroes up. The cask was then rolled out like a hogshead of sugar, placed in the wagon and driven off to Mulberry street. The colored heroes of this adventure may still be found at police headquarters, thankful to the ingenuity and daring of those who suggested and carried out this singular method of saving them from violence.'

———o———

Mr. Lincoln's Kind-Heartedness.

'An incident connected with Mr. Shultz illustrates the kind-heartedness of Mr. Lincoln On his return from his former imprisonment, on parole, young Shultz was sent to Camp Parole, at Alexandria. Having had no furlough since the war, efforts were made, without success, to get him liberty to pay a brief visit to his friends; but having faith in the warm-heartedness of the President, the young soldier's widowed mother wrote to Mr. Lincoln, stating

that he had been in nearly every battle fought by the army
of the Potomac, had never asked a furlough, was now a
paroled prisoner, and in consequence unable to perform
active duties, that two of his brothers had also served in
the army, and asking that he be allowed to visit home,
that she might see him once more. Her trust in the President was not unfounded. He immediatoly caused a furlough to be given to her son, who, shortly before he was
exchanged, visited his family, to their great surprise and
joy.

———o———

" Dat's what Skeered 'em so bad!"

Says Lincoln, ' We were passing along the wharves a
few days ago, wondering at the amount of business that
was there transacted. While standing observing a cargo
of horses being transferred from a vessel to the shore, an
' old contraband' appeared at our elbow, touching his fur
hat, and scraping an enormous foot. He opened his battery upon us with the following :

' Well, boss, how is yer ?'

'Pretty well, daddy ; how are you ?'

' I'se fuss rate, I is. B'long to Old Burnemside's boys,
does yer ?'

' Yes, I belong to that party. Great boys, ain't they ?'

' Well I thought yer b'longed to dat party. Great man,
he is, dat's sartin. Yes, sir. We waited and waited ; we
heard yer was coming' but we mos guv yer up. 'Deed we
jest did ; but one mornin' we heard de big guns, way down
ribber, go bang, bang, bang, and de folks round yer began
to cut dar stick mitey short, and trabble up de rail track.

Den bress de good Lord, we knowed yer was coming, but we held our jaw. Bymeby de sojers begun to cut dar stick, too, and dey did trabble! Goramity, 'pears dey made de dirt fly! Ya, ha!'

'Why, were they scared so bad?'

'De sogers didn't skeer um so much as dem black boats. Kase, yer see, de sojers shot solid balls, and dey not mind dem so much; but when dem boats say b-o-o-m, dey knowd de *rotten balls* was comin, and they skeeted quicker'n a streak of litenin.'

'What! rotten balls did the boats throw at them?'

'Dont yer know? What, dem balls dat are bad, dar rotten; fly all to bits—'deed does dey—play de very debbil wid yer. No dodgin' dem dere balls: 'kase yer dunno whare dey fly too—strike yah and fly yandah; dat's what skeered 'em so bad!'

'Well, what are you going to do when the war's over?'

'Dunno, 'praps I goes Noff wid dis crowd. Pretty much so, I guess. 'Pears ter me dis child had better be movin'.'

———o———

The Darned Thing.

'The following was told of a soldier wounded by a shell from Fort Wagner. He was going to the rear with a mutilated arm.

'Wounded by a shell?' he was asked.

'Yes,' he coolly answered, 'I was right under the darned thing when the bottom dropped out.'

The President shaking hands with Wounded Rebels.

A correspondent, who was with the President on the occasion of his recent visit to Frederick, Md., tells the following incident:

'After leaving Gen. Richardson, the party passed a house in which was a large number of confederate wounded. By request of the President, the party alighted and entered the building. Mr. Lincoln, after looking, remarked to the wounded confederates that if they had no objection he would be pleased to take them by the hand. He said the solemn obligations which we owe to our country and posterity compel the prosecution of this war, and it followed that many were our enemies through uncontrollable circumstances and he bore them no malice, and could take them by the hand with sympathy and good feeling. After a short silence the confederates came forward, and each silently but fervently shook the hand of the President. Mr. Lincoln and Gen. McClellan then walked forward by the side of those who were wounded too severely to be able to arise, and bid them to be of good cheer ; assuring them that every possible care should be bestowed upon them to ameliorate their condition. It was a moving scene, and there was not a dry eye in the building, either among the nationals or confederates. Both the President and Gen. McClellan were kind in their remarks and treatment of the rebel sufferers during this remarkable interview.'

A Pedlar made to swallow his own Pies.

We have read frequent allusions to the rough points in
the character of General Nelson, who has succeeded, we
believe, to the command of Gen. Mitchell's division. The
following account of one of his performances sounds so
much like other things alleged of him, that we suspect it
may be accounted at least half true, and may not be out
of place in Old Abe's Jokes :

Gen. Nelson, the commander of our division, occasionally comes dashing through camp, bestowing a gratuitious
cursing to some offender and is off like a shot.   He is a
great, rough, profane old fellow—has followed the seas
many years.   He has a plain, good, old fashioned fire-
place kindness about him that is always shown to those
that do their duty.   But offenders meet with no mercy at
his hands.   The General hates pedlars.   There are many
that come about the camp selling hoe-cakes, pies, milk,
&c., at exorbitant prices.   Cracker-fed-soldiers are free
with their money ; they will pay ten times the value of an
article if they want it.   The other day the General came
across a pedlar selling something that he called pies, not
the delicious kind of pies that our Northern mothers make
—the very thought of which even now makes me home
sick—but an indigestible combination of flattened dough
and wolly peaches, minus sugar, minus spice, minus everything that is good—any of which the General swore
would kill a hyena deader than the devil.   'What do
you charge for those pies?' belched out the General.

Fifty cents apiece,' responded the pie-man.   ' Fifty cents

apiece, for pies,' roared the General. ' Now, you infernal
swindling pirate,' roared he, letting fly one of his great
rifled oaths, that fairly made the fellow tremble, ' I want
you to go to work and cram every one of those pies down
you as quick as the Lord will let you.   Double quick, you
villain.'   Expostulations, appeals, or promises were of no
avail, and the pedlar was forced, to the great amusement
of the soldiers, to down half a dozen of his own pies—all
he had left.   ' Now,' said the General to the fellow, after
he had finished his repast, and stood looking as death-like
as the certain doctor that was forced to swallow his own
medicine—' leave, and if ever I catch you back here
again, swindling my men, I'll hang you.'   The man de-
parted.

————o————

Old Abe occasionally Browses Around.

A party of gentlemen, among whom was a doctor of di-
vinity of great comeliness of manner called at the White
House, to pay their respects to the President.   On inquir-
ing for that dignitary, the servant informed them that the
President was at dinner, but he would present their
cards.   The doctor demurred to this, saying they would
not disturb Mr. Lincoln, but would call again.   Michael
persisted in assuring them it would make no difference to
the President, and bolted in with the cards.   In a few
minutes, the President walked into the room, with a kindly salutation, and a request that the friends would take
seats.   The doctor expressed his regret that their visit
was so ill-timed, and that his Excellency was disturbed
while at dinner.   ' O ! no consequence at all,' said the

good-natured Mr. Lincoln : 'Mrs. Lincoln is absent at present, and when she is away, I generally browse around.'

———o———

Mr. Lincoln and the Barber.

The other day a distinguished public officer was at Washington, and in an interview with the President, introduced the question of slavery emancipation. 'Well, you see,' said Mr. Lincoln, 'we've got to be mighty cautious how we manage the negro question. If we're not we shall be like the barber out in Illinois, who was shaving a fellow with a hatchet face and lantern jaws like mine. The barber stuck his finger in his customer's mouth to make his cheek stick out, but while shaving away he cut through the fellow's cheek and cut off his own finger! If we don't play mighty smart about the nigger we shall do as the barber did.'

———o———

Old Abe on the " Compromise."

When the conversation turned upon the discussions as to the Missouri Compromise, it elicited the following quaint remark from the President : 'It used to amuse me some (sic) to find that the slave holders wanted more territory, because they had not room enough for their slaves, and yet they complained of not having the slave trade, because they wanted more slaves for their room.'

Old Abe on Banks' Expedition.

When Gen. Banks was fitting out his expedition to New Orleans, it will be remembered that the Preident used to answer all questions as to its destination with great frankness, by saying that it was going South.

————o————

Sufficient Cause for Furlough.

President Lincoln received the following pertinent letter from an indignant private, which speaks for itself: " Dear President—I have been in the service eighteen months, and 1 have never received a cent. I desire a furlough for fifteen days, in order to return home and remove my family to the poor house.' The President granted the furlough. It's a good story and true.

————o————

The President on " Mud."

By special permission of the ' Censor of the Press,' we are allowed to mention that the President, on alighting from his carriage, after his late Aquia Creek excursion, remarked, ' that it was all nonsense to say Virginia was disaffected, as he had found it a Clay State up to the hub.'

Lincoln on his Cabinet " Help."

A prominent senator was remonstrating with Mr. Lincoln a few days ago about keeping Mr. Chase in his Cabinet, when it was well known that Mr. C. is opposed, tooth and nail, to Mr. Lincoln's re-election.

'Now, see here,' said the President, 'when I was elected I resolved to hire my four Presidential rivals, pay them their wages, and be their 'boss.' These were Seward, Chase, Cameron and Bates ; but I got rid of Cameron after he had played himself out. As to discharging Chase or Seward, don't talk of it. I pay them their wages and am their boss, wouldn't let either of them out on the loose for the fee simple of the Almaden patent.'

————o————

Mr. Lincoln and the Millerite.

A gentleman, it is said, sometime ago hinted to the President that it was deemed quite settled that he would accept a re-nomination for his present office. whereupon Mr. Lincoln was reminded of a story of Jesse Dubois, out in Illinois. Jesse, as State Auditor, had charge of the State House at Springfield. An itinerant preacher came along and asked the use of it for a lecture. ' On what subject ?' asked Jesse. ' On the second coming of our Saviour,' answered the long-faced Millerite. ' Oh, bosh,' retorted uncle Jesse, testily, ' I guess if our Saviour had ever been to Springfield, and had got away with his life, he'd be too smart to think of coming back again.' This, Mr. Lincoln said, was very much his case about the succession.

A Good One by Old Abe.

The President is rather vain of his height, but one day
a young man called on him who was certainly three inches
taller than the former; he was like the mathematical
definition of the straight line, length without breadth.
'Really,' said Mr. Lincoln, 'I must look up to you; if you
ever get into a deep place you ought to be able to wade
out.

————o————

Tanning Leather.

During the siege of Vicksburg, several politicians called
upon General Grant to talk about political matters. Gen.
Grant listened to them for a few moments, and then interrupted them, saying: 'There is no use of talking about
politics to me. I know nothing about the subject, and
furthermore, I don't know of any person among my acquaintance who does. But there is one subject with which I am
acquainted, talk of that, and I am your man,' 'What is
that, General?' asked the politicians, in surprise. 'Tan-
ning leather,' replied General Grant. General Grant's
father was a wealthy tanner out west, before the rebellion,
and the General assisted in conducting the business.

Southern "Happiness."

Old Abe declares, in epigrammatic phase, ' the only happy people in the Confederacy are those who have black hearts or black skins.'

Reduced to plainer English, this confession means that the rebel rulers and the rebel speculators are all rascals together, and that the blacks are never happy until they begin to run away from such contaminating influences.

————o————

Lincoln's Advice.

President Lincoln is not so far weighed down by the cares of his office that he cannot still tell a good story. He is greatly bothered, as a matter of course, by men who have got some patent plan for conqueriing the rebels. One man has an invention which, if applied to our ships, will enable them to batter down every rebel fort on the entire southern coast. Another has a river gunboat, which can sail straight down the Mississippi, without the fear of a rebel shell or ball, and so on. A few days ago a western farmer sought the President day after day, until he procured the much-desired audience. He, too, had a plan for the successful prosecution of the war, to which Mr. Lincoln listened as patiently as he could. When he was through, he asked the opinion of the President upon his plan. ' Well,' said Mr. Lincoln, ' I'll answer by telling you a story. You have heard of Mr. Blank, of Chicago? He was an immense loafer in his way, in fact, never did anything in his life. One day he got crazy over a great rise in the price of wheat upon which many wheat speculators gained large fortunes. Blank started off one morning to one of the most successful of the wheat speculators, and with much enthusiasm laid before him a ' plan' by which he, the said Blank, was certain of becoming independently rich. When he had finished, he asked the opinion of his hearer upon his plan of operations. The reply came as follows : ' My advice is that you *stick to your business.*' ' But,' asked Blank, ' what is my business ?' ' I don't know, I'm sure, what it is,' says the merchant, ' but *whatever it is I would advise you to stick to it!*' And now, said Mr. Lincoln, ' I mean nothing offensive, for I know you mean well, but I think you had better stick to your business and leave the war to those who have the responsibility of managing it !' Whether the former was satisfied or not I cannot say, but he did not tarry long in the Presidential mansion.

———o———

Old Abe Appoints a General.

One of the new levies of troops required the appointment of a large additional number of Brigadier and Major Generals. Among the immense number of applications, Mr. Lincoln came upon one wherein the claims of a certain worthy (not in the service at all) ' for a generalship' were glowingly set forth. But the applicant didn't specify whether he wanted to be Brigadier or Major General. The President observed this difficulty, and solved it by a lucid endorsement. The clerk, on receiving the paper again, found written across its back, 'Major General, I reckon. A. Lincoln.'

————o————

A Practical Joke, not exactly Old Abe's, however.

Quite a commotion was created in a Bleecker street boarding-house by the arrest of two Southern gentlemen, Messrs. Joyce and Richardson, of Baltimore, for violating their parole and returning to the North, after having been sent to Dixie. On the occasion of their last arrest, several ladies, residing at their boarding-house, used some very expressive language, and rather tersely expressed their " feelinks" on the—to them—outrageous manner the government sought to vindicate its authority. Doubtless, all the women were perfectly loyal, and each would gladly take the oath of allegiance to the government, or " any other man ;" but evidently some sarcastic old gentleman did not believe it, and in order to test the question concocted the following letter, which was duly directed and forwarded to the lady of whom he appeared most suspicious :

Headquarters U. S. Army,
No. —— —— street,
New York, February --, 1864.

Mrs. —— is respectfully requested to call at the above headquarters within six days, for examination on matters of importance which will then be stated to her.

By Order of the Military Department,
A. S. JONES,
Assistant Adj.-General.

Bring this notice with you.

On receipt of this notice, the lady, to whom it was addressed, began to feel some misgivings. The oftener she read the mandate the more nervous she became, until at length, like a woman of spirit, she determined to present herself before the " powers that be," and await whatever explanation might be given. Conscious that in no act or deed had she been a disloyal woman, she felt certain that if the military authorities had any knowledge of the words she had made use of on the occasion referred to, they would overlook the hasty expressions of an affectionate nature, excited by the midnight arrest of those whom she had hitherto looked upon as peaceful, law-abiding citizens. Accordingly, the lady visited at the number indicated in the note, but discovered there no signs of military headquarters. On the next block, in the same street, were the headquarters of General Dix. Determined to have a clear record, the lady proceeded thither. Being stopped by the sentinel, she requested an audience with General Dix, and in due course found herself in the presence of that polite and patriotic officer. The interview was substantially as follows :

Lady : I called, sir, to know what this letter means.

General (after reading the document, smiling) : My dear Madam, I am quite as ignorant as you seem to be. There is no such person as A. S. Jones on my staff, or to my knowledge connected with the military forces of the United States, at present on duty in this city.

Lady (very much relieved) : I thought so, sir, but I meant to be certain. I believe I have been hoaxed, sir, because I am from Baltimore, and resided at the house where Mr. Joyce was recently arrested. Some wicked person has sent me this to annoy me.

General : Doubtless that is the case, Madam, but I don't see that I can help you.

Lady : I wish you could. I declare I would get you to send a file of soldiers after the scamp that has sent this message to me.

General (smiling) : That would indeed be an arbitrary arrest that I cannot be a party to ; and your only remedy, that I see, is to be patient, until, perhaps, the individual himself shows his hand, and then you may punish him through the civil law.

Lady : Thank you, General. I am sorry I have troubled you, but I felt anxious to appear right in the matter.

General : No apologies, my dear Madam.

Thereupon, the General bowed the lady out, and, perhaps, smiled inwardly at her confusion, as he proceeded to transact his usual business. It is unnecessary to describe the feelings of the lady as she joyfully wended her way homeward, and our reporter drops the curtain upon the scenes in a certain private room of that boarding-house, when Mrs. W—— revealed to her confidential friends how she had been the victim of a practical joke. A rod is being pickled for the practical joker, and it will be surprising if a woman's wit does not find some means of applying it to the back of the mean-spirited hound.

———o———

Old Abe and His Tod.

'For occasional sallies of genuine original wit, give us a country grocery on winter evenings and rainy days, and the bar rooms of country hotels. As an instance take the following, which occurred in a bar-room. There was quite a collection, and our friend S., who is a democrat, and friend M., who is a republican, had been earnestly but pleasantly discussing politics; and as a lull took place in the conversation, S. spoke up as follows :

' M., how many public men are there who are *really* temperance men ?'

' Oh, I don't know,' replied M.

' Well,' said S., ' I don't know of but one that I can speak positively of on *our* side, and that is General Cass.'

' Well,' said M , promptly, ' there is President Lincoln on *our* side, certain.'

' Guess not,' said L., incredulously.

' Guess yes,' replied M., warmly.

' But you don't pretend to say that President Lincoln is a temperance man,' asked S.

' Yes, I do,' answered M., ' and can maintain the statement.'

' Well, now I tell you that Abraham Lincoln is as fond of his tod as any man living,' replied S., earnestly, ' and I can prove it to you.'

' Well, I tell you that he isn't,' replied M., who began to get excited ; ' that he is as pure and strict a temperance man as there is in the country.'

' I contend,' replied S.' with provoking coolness, ' that Abraham Lincoln is so fond of his tod that it is the last thing he thinks of when he goes to bed, and the first when he wakes in the morning.'

'It's a confounded *locofoco lie !*' exclaimed M., springing
to his feet.

'Hold on, friend M.,' said S., 'what was Lincoln's
wife's name before she was married ?'

'*Todd, by thunder!*' exclaimed M., jumping more than a
foot from the floor; 'boy's let's adjourn to the other
room.'

————o————

Pluck to the Toe-Nail.

'A wag thus describes the constitution of his company
of volunteers:

'I'm captain of the Baldinsville company. I riz grad-
ooaly but majesticly from drummer's secrĕtary to my present position. I determined to have my company composed
excloosively of offissers, everybody to rank as brigadier-
general. As all air commandin' offissers there ain't no
jelusy ; and as we air all exceedin' smart, it t'aint worth
while to try to outstrip each other. The idee of a company composed excloosively of commanders-in-chief orrig-
gernated I spose I skursely need say, in this brane. Considered as an idee, I flatter myself it's pretty heffy.—
We've got the tackticks at our tongs' end, but what we
pareickly excel in is restin' muskits. We can rest muskits with anybody. Our corpse will do its dooty. We'll
be chopt into sassiage meet before we'll exhibit our coat
tails to the foe. We'll fight till there's nothing left to us
but our little toes, and even they shall defiently wriggle.'

The National Joker and the Nigger Mathematician.

A gentleman, who happened to have an interview with the national joker just previous to the battle of Gettysburg, ventured to turn the conversation on the rebel invasion of Pennsylvania, and made the remark that the rebels were splendidly armed. ' There's no doubt of that,' replied Mr. Lincoln, ' because we supplied them with the best we had.' The visitor expressed a confident hope, however, that Meade would be able to beat Lee and·capture his whole army. The President grinned to the utmost extent of his classic mouth, and remarked that he was afraid there would be too much ' nigger mathematics ' in it. The visitor smiled at the allusion, as he felt bound in politeness to do, supposing that there must be something in it, though he could not see the point. ' But I suppose you don't know what nigger mathematics is,' continued Mr. Lincoln. ' Lay down your hat for a minute, and I'll tell you.' He himself resumed the sitting posture, leaned back in his chair, elevated his heels on the table, and went on with his story. ' There was a darkey in my neighborhood called Pompey, who, from a certain quickness in figuring up the prices of chickens and vegetables, got the reputation of being a mathematical genius. Mr. Johnson, a darkey preacher, heard of Pompey, and called to see him. Hear ye're a great mat'm'tishun, Pompey. Yes, sar, you jus try. Well, Pompey, I'ze compound a problem in mat'matics. All right, sar. Now, Pompey, s'pose der am tree pigeons sittin on a rail fence, and you fire a gun at 'em and shoot one, how many's left ? Two, ob coors,

replies Pompey, after a little wool-scratching. Ya, ya, ya,
laughs Mr. Johnson ; I knowed you was a fool, Pompey ;
dere's none left ; one's dead, and d'udder two's flown
away. That's what makes me say,' continued Mr. Lincoln,
' that I'm afraid there will be too much nigger mathematics in the Pennsylvania campaign.' And the result
showed that, in this instance at least, the anecdote suited
the fact. Lee's army was the three pigeons. One of them
was taken down at Gettysburg, but the other two flew off
over the Potomac.

————o————

Big Brindle and the Highfalutin Colonel.

President Lincoln tells the following story of Col. W
who had been elected to the Legislature, and had also
been judge of the county court. His elevation, however,
had made him somewhat pompous, and he became very
fond of using big words. On his farm he had a very
large and mischievous ox called ' Big Brindle,' which frequently broke down his neighbors' fences, and committed
other depredations, much to the Colonel's annoyance.

One morning after breakfast in the presence of Mr.
Lincoln who had stayed with him over night, and who
was on his way to town, he called his overseer and said
to him :

'Mr. Allen, I desire you to impound Big Brindle, in
order that I may hear no animadversions on his eternal
depredations.

Allen bowed and walked off, sorely puzzled to know
what the Colonel meant. So after Col. W. left for town,

he went to his wife and asked her what Col. W. meant by telling him to impound the ox.

'Why, he meant to tell you to put him in a pen,' said she.

Allen left to perform the feat, for it was no inconsiderable one, as the animal was very wild and vicious, and after a great deal of trouble and vexation succeeded.

'Well,' said he, wiping the perspiration from his brow, and soliloquizing, 'this is impounding, is it? Now, I am dead sure that the Colonel will ask me if I impounded Big Brindle, and I'll bet I puzzle him as he did me.

The next day the Colonel gave a dinner party, and as he was not aristocratic, Mr. Allen, the overseer, sat down with the company. After the second or third glass was discussed, the Col. turned to the overseer and said :

'Eh, Mr. Allen, did you impound Big Brindle, sir?'

Allen straightened himself, and looking around at the company said :

'Yes, I did, sir, but old Brindle transcended the impannel of the impound, and scatterlophisticated all over the equanimity of the forest.'

The company burst into an immoderate fit of laughter, while the Colonel's face reddened with discomfiture.

'What do you mean by that, sir?' said the Colonel.

'Why, I mean, Colonel,' said Allen, 'That old Brindle, being prognosticated with an idea of the cholera, ripped and tared, snorted and pawed dirt, jumped the fence, tuck to the woods, and would not be impounded no how.'

This was too much; the company roared again, in which the Colonel was forced to join, and in the midst of the laughter Allen left the table, saying to himself as he went,

"I reckon the Colonel won't ask me to impound any more oxen.'

————o————

Lincoln and the Lost Apple.

'On a late occasion when the White House was open to the public, a farmer from one of the border counties of Virginia, told the President that the Union soldiers, in passing his farm, had helped themselves not only to hay, but his horse, and he hoped the President would urge the proper officer to consider his claim immediately.

'Why, my dear sir,' replied Mr. Lincoln, blandly, 'I couldn't think of such a thing. If I consider individual cases, I should find work enough for twenty Presidents.'

Bowie urged his needs persistently ; Mr. Lincoln declined good naturedly.

'But,' said the persevering sufferer, ' couldn't you just give me a line to Col. —— about it? just one line!'

'Ha, ha, ha!' responded the amiable Old Abe, shaking himself fervently, and crossing his legs the other way, 'that reminds me of old Jack Chase, out in Illinois,'

At this the crowd huddled forward to listen :

'You've seen Jack—I know him like a brother—used to be lumberman on the Illinois, and he was steady and sober, and the best raftsman on the river. It was quite a trick twenty-five years ago, to take the logs over the rapids, but he was skillful with a raft and always kept her straight in the channel. Finally a steamer was put on, and Jack—he's dead now, poor fellow !—was made captain of her. He always used to take the wheel, going through the rapids. One day when the boat was plunging and wallowing along the boiling current, and Jack's utmost vigilance was being exercised to keep her in the narrow channel, a boy pulled his coat-tail and hailed him with: 'Say, Mister Captain! I wish you would just stop your boat a minute—I've lost my apple overboard!'

————o————

Enlisting Negroes in the Union Army.

A slaveholder from the country approached an old acquaintance, also a slaveholder, residing in Nashville, the other day, and said:

'I have several negro men lurking about here somewhere. I wish you would look out for them, and when you find them do with them as if they were your own.'

'Certainly I will,' replied his friend.

A few days ago the parties met again, and the planter asked:

'Have you found my slaves?'

'I have.'

'And where are they?'

'Well, you told me to do with them just as if they were my own, and, as I made my men enlist in the Union army I did the same with yours.'

The astonished planter absquatulated.

————o————

"Old Abe" on Temperance.

The Twenty-first anniversary of the 'Sons of Temperance' was appropriately celebrated in Washington. The 'Sons' on reaching the White House, were invited to enter the East room, which was nearly filled by the ladies and gentlemen participating in the ceremonies. President Lincoln, on entering, was enthusiastically applauded, and, in the course of his response to the address presented to him, said that when he was a young man, long ago, before the Sons of Temperance, as an organization, had an existence, he in an humble way made Temperance speeches, and he thought he might say to this day he had never by his example belied what he then said. As to the suggestions for the purpose of the abandonment of the cause of temperance, he could not now respond to them. To prevent intemperance in the army is even a great part of the rules and articles of war. It is a part of the law of the land, and was so he presumed long ago, to dismiss officers for drunkenness. He was not sure that, consistently with the public service, more can be done than has been done. All, therefore, that he could promise, was to have a copy of the address submitted to the principal departments, and have it considered whether it contains any suggestions which will improve the cause of temperance, and repress drunkenness in the army any better than it is already done. He thought the reasonable men of the world had long since agreed that intemperance was one of the greatest, if not the very greatest, of all the evils among mankind. That was not a matter of dispute. All men agreed that intemperance was a great curse, but differed about the cure. The suggestion that it existed to a great extent was true, whether it was a cause of defeat he knew not; but he did know that there was a good deal of it on the other side. Therefore they had no right to beat us on that ground. (Laughter.) The remarks of the President were listened to with great interest and repeatedly interrupted by applause.

———o———

How Bean Hackett was made a Zouave.

I was put through a rigid course of examination before I could be made a Zouave, and I say it with feelings of gratification and self-esteem that I was remarkably well posted in the catechism. My father was a hero of the revolution, having been caught once in a water-wheel, and whirled around rapidly a number of times. Others of the family have also distinguished themselves as military men at different periods, but their deeds of courage are too well-known to need repetition.

The following is a copy *verbatim et literatim et wordem* of most of the questions propounded to me and the answers thereto, which my intimate acquaintance with the Army Regulations and the Report of the Committee on the Conduct of the War enable me to answer readily and accurately. My interrogator was a little man in Federal blue, with gold leaves on his shoulders. They called him Major, but he looked young enough to be a minor. He led off with—

'How old are you, and what are your qualifications ?'

'Twenty-two, and a strong stomach.'

Then I requested him to fire his interrogations singly, which he did.

'What is the first duty to be learned by a soldier ?'

'How to draw his rations.'

'What is the most difficult feat for a soldier to perform ?'

'Drawing his bounty.'

' If you were in the rear rank of a company during an action, and the man in the front rank before you should be wounded and disabled, what would you do ?'

' I would despatch myself to the rear for a surgeon immediately. Some men would step forward and take the wounded man's place, but that is unnatural.'

' If you were commanding skirmishers, and saw cavalry advancing in the front and infantry in the rear, which would you meet ?'

' Neither ; I would mass myself for a bold movement, and shove out sideways.'

' If you were captured, what line of conduct would you pursue ?

' I would treat my captors with the utmost civility.'

' What are the duties of Home Guards ?'

' Their duty is to see that they have no duties.'

' What will you take ?'

——' Bourbon, straight !'"

————o————

Uncle Abe and the Judge.

' In the conversation which occurred before dinner, I was amused to observe the manner in which Mr. Lincoln used the anecdotes for which he is so famous. Where men bred in courts, accustomed to the world, or versed in diplomacy, would use some subterfuge, or would make a polite speech, or give a shrug of the shoulders as the means of getting out of an embarrassing position, Mr. Lincoln raises a laugh by some bold west-country anecdote, and moves off in the cloud of merriment produced by the joke. Thus, when Mr. Bates was remonstrating apparently against the appointment of some indifferent lawyer to a place of judicial importance, the President interposed with, ' Come, now, Bates, he's not half as bad as you think. Besides that, I must tell you, he did me a good turn long ago. When I took to the law, I was going to court one morning, with some ten or twelve miles of bad road before me, and I had no horse. The judge overtook me in his wagon. 'Hallo, Lincoln! are you not going to the court-house. Come in and I will give you a seat.' Well, I got in, and the judge went on reading his papers. Presently the wagon struck a stump on one side of the road; then it hopped off to the other. I looked out, and I saw the driver was jerking from side to side in his seat : so says I, ' Judge, I think your coachman has been taking a little drop too much this morning.' ' Well, I declare, Lincoln,' said he, ' I should not much wonder if you are right, for he has nearly upset me half-a-dozen times since starting.' So, putting his head out of the window, he shouted, ' Why, you infernal scoundrel, you are drunk !' Upon which pulling up his horses, and turning round with great gravity, the coachman said, ' By gorra ! that's the first rightful decision that you have given for the last twelve month.' While the company were laughing, the President beat a quiet retreat from the neighborhood of the Attorney-General.

————o————

The liberal and patriotic citizen who has been drafted has purchased a gun which he says is very sure to go off—on another man's shoulders.

Mince Pies vs. Tracts.

The President says his political friends often remind him of the following story :

A rebel lady visited the hospital at Nashville one morning with a negro servant, who carried a large basket on his arm, covered with a white linen cloth.   She approached a German and accosted him thus :

' Are you a good Union man ?'

' I ish dat,' was the laconic reply of the German, at the same time casting a hopeful glance at the aforesaid basket.

' That is all I wanted to know,' replied the lady, and beckoning to the negro to follow, she passed to the opposite side of the room, where a rebel soldier lay, and asked him the same question, to which he very promptly replied : 'Not by d—d sight.'   The lady thereupon uncovered the basket and laid out a bottle of wine, mince pies, pound cake and other delicacies, which were greedily devoured in the presence of the Union soldiers who felt somewhat indignant.

On the following morning, however, another lady made her appearance with a large covered basket, and she also accosted our German friend, and desired to know if he was a Union man.

' I ish, by Got ; I no care what you got; I bese Union.'

The lady set the basket on the table, and our German friend thought the truth availed in this case, if it did fail in the other.   But imagine the length of the poor fellow's face when the lady uncovered the basket and presented him with about a bushel of tracts. He shook his head dolefully and said :

'I no read English, und, peside dat rebel on 'se oder side of 'se house need tem so more as me.'

The lady distributed them and left.

Not long afterwards along came another richly dressed lady, who propounded the same question to the German. He stood gazing at the basket apparently at a loss for a reply. At length he answered her in Yankee style, as follows :

'By Got, you no got me dis time ; vot you got mit the basket ?'

The lady required an unequivocal reply to her question, and was about to move on when our German friend shouted out :

'If you got tracts, I bese Union ; but if you got mince pie mit pound cake unt vine, I be sesech like de tibel.'

Soldiers have little deire to read tracts when they are famished for the want of those little delicacies so conducive to the recovery of hospital patients.   When our ladies visit hospitals with tracts, we should suggest the importance of accompanying them with a basket of provisions ; they will be better appreciated.

————o————

The Niggers and the Small Pox.

I dropped in upon Mr. Lincoln and found him busily counting greenbacks. "This, sir,' said he, 'is something out of my usual line ; but a President of the United States has a multiplicity of duties not specified in the Constitution or acts of Congress. This is one of them. This money belongs to a poor negro who is a porter in one of the Departments (the Treasury), and who is at present very bad with the small pox. He did not catch it from me, however ; at least I think not. He is now in hospital, and could not draw his pay because he could not sign his name.

I have been at considerable trouble to overcome the difficulty and get it for him, and have at length succeeded in cutting red tape, as you newspaper men say. I am now dividing the money and putting by a portion labeled, in an envelope, with my own hands, according to his wish;' and his Excellency proceeded to endorse the package very carefully. No one who witnessed the transaction could fail to appreciate the goodness of heart which would prompt a man who is borne down by the weight of cares unparalleled in the world's history, to turn aside for a time from them to succor one of the humblest of his fellow creatures in sickness and sorrow.

————o————

Why Lincoln didn't stop the War.

The soldiers at Helena, in Arkansas, used to amuse the inhabitants of that place, on their first arrival, by telling them yarns, of which the following is a sample :

'Some time ago Jeff Davis got tired of the war, and invited President Lincoln to meet him on neutral ground to discuss terms of peace. They met accordingly, and after a talk concluded to settle the war by dividing the territory and stopping the fighting. The North took the

Northern States, and the South the Gulf and seaboard
Southern States.   Lincoln took Texas and Missouri, and
Davis Kentucky and Tennessee; so that all were parceled
off excepting Arkansas.   Lincoln didn't want it—Jeff.
wouldn't have it, neither would consent to take it, and on
that they split; and the war has been going on ever
since.'

-----o-----

Lincoln's Estimate of the " Honors."

As a further elucidation of Mr. Lincoln's estimate of
Presidential honors, a story is told of how a supplicant
for office, of more than ordinary pretentions, called upon
him, and, presuming on the activity he had shown in behalf of the Republican ticket, asserted as a reason why
the office should be given to him, that he had made Mr.
Lincoln President.

" You made me President, did you?' said Mr. Lincoln,
with a twinkle of his eye.   ' I think I did,' said the applicant.   ' Then a pretty mess you've got me into, that's all,'
replied the President, and closed the discussion.

-----o-----

Pring up de Shackasses, for Cot sake !

President Lincoln often laughed over the following incident : One of General Fremont's batteries of eight Parrot
guns, supported by a squadron of horse commanded by
Major Richards, was in a sharp conflict with a battery
of the enemy near at hand, and shells and shot were flying
thick and fast, when the commander of the battery, a

German, one of Fremont's staff, rode suddenly up to the cavalry, exclaiming, in loud and excited terms, ' Pring up de shackasses, pring up de shackasses, for Cot sake, hurry up de shackasses im-me-di-ate-ly.' The necessity of this order, though not quite apparent, will be more obvious when it is remembered that the ' shackasses ' are mules, carrying mountain howitzers, which are fired from the backs of that much-abused but valuable animal ; and the immediate occasion for the ' shackasses ' was that two regiments of rebel infantry were at that moment discovered descending a hill immediately behind our batteries. The ' shackasses," with the howitzers loaded with grape and canister, were soon on the ground. The mules squared themselves, as they well knew how, for the shock. A terrific volley was poured into the advancing column, which immediately broke and retreated. Two hundred and seventy-eight dead bodies were found in the ravine next day, piled closely together as they fell, the effects of that volley from the backs of the ' shackasses."

--------o--------

Abe's Long Legs.

When the President landed at Aquia Creek, going to see Burnside, there were boards in the way on the wharf, which the men hastened to remove, but the President remarked, in his usual style, ' Never mind, boys; my legs are pretty long, have brought me thus far through life and I think they will take me over this difficulty.'

The President and " Banks."

Loquitur an eminent Pennsylvania Congressman : ' Sir, Banks is a failure, isn't he ?'

' Well, that is harsh,' responds the President ; ' but he *hasn't* come up to my expectations.'

' Then, sir, why don't you remove him ?'

' Well, sir, one principal reason is, that *it would hurt General Banks' feelings very much !'*

———o———

Old Abe's Noble Saying.

' President Lincoln says many homely things and many funny things. His speech at the late ceremony in honor of the dead at Gettysburg proves that he can also say noble and beautiful things. Is not the following extract worthy, in its touching simplicity, of being handed down to the ages among the great sayings of great men :—' *The world will little note nor long remember what we say here, but they can never forget what they did here.'*

———o———

" Where the D——l are the Buggies."

' The citizens of a small city in Pennsylvania, being thrown into considerable excitement by reason of the report that the rebels under Lee were advancing upon them, held a meeting for the purpose of organizing themselves into a regiment. During the organization of the regiment, the question of arms, ammunition, etc., was being discussed, when an old gentleman, very much excited, and

towering head and shoulders above the crowd, exclaimed,
in a stentorian voice : 'Are there not any cannons to de-
fend the city ?'

Voice from the crowd—' Yes, but they are not mounted.'

Old Gent—' Why ain't they mounted.'

Voice from the crowd—' Because we have no carriages.'

Old Gent—(Still louder and more excited)—'Then,
where the devil are the buggies ?'

———o———

"I Mean 'Honest Old Abe.'"

' A good story is told of an old Cleveland deacon, who
just after Lincoln started on his journey for Washington,
went to an evening prayer meeting, and being somewhat
in a hurry, went down immediately on his knees, and made
an earnest prayer in behalf of the President of the United
States, asking that God would strengthen him and bless
him in all his undertakings. Rising from his knees he left
the church, apparently having an earnest call elsewhere.
Presently he returned in a great hurry, and plumping
again on his knees, thus addressed himself; ' Oh, Lord, it
may be as well for me to add as an explanation to my
prayer just uttered, that by the President of the United
States I mean honest old Abe Lincoln, and not that other
chap who is yet sitting in the national nest, and for whom
I don't care shucks. Amen.'

Old Abe " C's " it.

' I consoled the President this morning by relating to him what an unfortunate letter ' C ' was in the Presidential *Chase*. A joke—do you take ? I related the fate of Crawford, Calhoun, Clay and Cass. The Presidential eye brightened up. I saw hope displayed in every lineament of his countenance. He replied, ' I *see* it.' How quick he is at *repartee*. How pointed, too. I think the Presidential heart has beat easier since the administry of my last solace.'

————o————

Lincoln's Ideas about Slavery.

The story will be remembered, perhaps, of Mr. Lincoln's reply to a Springfield (Ill.) clergyman, who asked him what was to be his policy on the slavery question.

' Well, your question is rather a cool one, but I will answer it by telling you a story. You know Father B., the old Methodist preacher ? and you know Fox river and its freshets ? Well, once in the presence of Father B., a young Methodist was worrying about Fox river, and expressing fears that he should be prevented from fulfilling some of his appointments by a freshet in the river. Father B. checked him in his gravest manner. Said he : ' Young man, I have always made it a rule in my life not to cross Fox river till I get to it !' 'And,' said the President, ' I am not going to worry myself over the slavery question till I get to it.' A few days afterwards a Methodist minister called on the President, and on being

)resented to him, said simply : ' Mr. President, I have come to tell you that I think we have got to Fox river !' Mr. Lincoln thanked the clergyman and laughed heartily.

————o————

Abe and the Distance to the Capitol.

It is stated that he was much disgusted at the crowd of officers who sometime ago used to loiter about the Washington hotels, and he is reported to have remarked to a member of Congress : ' These fellows and the Congressmen do vex me sorely.' Another member of Congress was conversing with the President, and was somewhat annoyed by the President's propensity to divert attention from the serious subject he had on his mind by ludicrous allusions. 'Mr. Lincoln,' said he, 'I think you would have your joke if you were within a mile of hell.' ' Yes, sir, that is about the distance to the Capitol.'

————o————

Abe thinks T. R. Strong, but Coffee are stronger.

It is told by an intelligent contraband, who is probably reliable, that Mr. Lincoln was walking up Pennsylvania avenue the other day, relating ' a little story' to Secretary Seward, when the latter called his attention to a new sign bearing the name of ' T. R. Strong.' ' Ha !' says old Abe his countenance lighting up with a peculiar smile, ' T. R. Strong, but coffee are stronger.' Seward smiled, but made no reply.

Putting Salt on the Monitor's Tail.

War is a pretty serious business ; but they are not always gloomy at the War Department.   When the foolish rumor was current in Washington that the Monitor had been captured, the President walked over to the War Department and asked whether the report ws true.

' Certainly,' replied an officer with due gravity.

'How did the rebels succeed in capturing her ?' asked the President.

' By putting salt on her tail,' was the reply.

The President's only answer was, ' I owe you one.'

————o————

Old Abe Never Heard of it Before.

Some moral philosoper was telling the President one day about the undercurrent of public opinion.   He went on to explain at length, and drew an illustration from the Mediterranean Sea.   The current seemed very curiously to flow in both from the Black Sea and the Atlantic Ocean, but a shrewd Yankee, by means of a contrivance of floats, had discovered that at the outlet into the Atlantic only about thirty feet of the surface water flowed inward, while there was a tremenduous current under that flowing out.   ' Well,' said Mr. Lincoln, much bored, ' that don't remind me of any story I ever heard of.'   The philosopher despaired of making a serious impression by his argument, and left.

Why Lincoln Appointed Fremont.

General Fremont stood a very small chance of being assigned to a command. But fortunately for him, the President one morning read in a Washington paper the speech of Col. Blair, M. C., upon the late commander in Missouri. The President having attentively perused it, said to some one near him, ' Oh, this will never do ; it's persecution.' He put the paper in his pocket, walked over to the War Department, and in less than half an hour Major-General Fremont was appointed to the command of the Mountain Department.

————o————

Father Abraham's Good Clothes.

At the beginning of the war John Perry, then a resident of Georgia, was compelled to take the oath of allegiance to the Southern Confederacy and agreed not to bear arms against it. He removed to West Troy soon afterwards and in September was drafted. Before the time of his appearance at Albany he wrote to the Provost Marshal General, Colonel Fry, stating the dilemma, and asking whether he could not be released from his obligation to serve Uncle Sam. The reply of Col. Fry has just been received. He states that he fully appreciates Mr. Perry's position, and has no idea of making him violate his oath. He kindly consents, therefore, that the conscript Perry shall be sent to the Northwest to fight Indians; but he can't for a moment think of absolving him from wearing ' Father Abraham's good clothes.'

————o————

The President says that Jeff is on his Last Legs.

Because we gave him the grant (Grant) of Vicksburg and he couldn't hold it; we gave him the banks (Banks) of Port Hudson and they destroyed his best gardner (Gardner) and all he raised during the last two years; we gave him mead (Meade) at Gettysburg and he couldn't swallow it; we have his best wagoner (Wagner) fast at Charleston; compelled him to haul in his brag (Bragg) and get in the lee (Lee) of his rebel army.

————o————

Old Abe on the Congressmen.

As the President and a friend were sitting on the House of Representatives steps, the session closed, and the members filed out in a body. Abraham looked after them with a sardonic smile.

' That reminds me,' said he, 'of a little incident. When I was quite a boy, my flat-boat lay up at Alton, on the Mississippi, for a day, and I strolled about the town. I saw a large stone building, with massive walls, not so handsome, though, as this; and while I was looking at it, the iron gateway opened, and a great body of men came out. ' What do you call that?' I asked a by-stander. 'That,' said he, ' is the State Prison, and those are all thieves, going home. Their time is up.'

General Viele and a Female Rebel.

General Egbert L. Viele, Governor of Norfolk, was visited one day by a lady. He noticed that she wore the confederate colors prominently in the shape of a brooch, and mildly suggested that it would, perhaps, have been in better taste to come to his office without such a decoration. 'I have a right, sir, to consult my own wishes as to what I shall wear.' 'Then, madam,' replied the General, 'permit me to claim an equal right in choosing with whom I shall converse.' And the dignified lady had to withdraw from his presence.

————o————

Lincoln on Vice and Virtue.

Some one was smoking in the presence of the President, and complimented him on having no vices, neither drinking nor smoking. 'That is a doubtful compliment,' answered the President ; ' I recollect once being outside a stage in Illinois, and a man sitting by me offered me a segar. I told him I had no vices. He said nothing, smoked for some time, and then grunted out, It's my experience that folks who have no vices have plagued few virtues.'

————o————

Potomac ! Bottomic ! ! Buttermilk

An amusing story is told by Old Abe of the ' Iowa First,' about the changes which a certain password underwent about the time of the battle of Springfield. One of

the Dubuque officers, whose duty it was to furnish the
guards with a password for the night, gave the word
' Potomac ' A German on guard, not understanding distinctly the difference between B's and P's, understood it
to be ' Bottomic,' and this, on being transferred to another, was corrupted to ' Buttermilk.' Soon afterward, the
officer who had given the word wished to return through
the lines, and on approaching a sentinel was ordered to
halt and the word demanded. He gave ' Potomac.'
' Nicht right—you don't pass mit me dis way.' ' But this
is the word, and I will pass.' ' No, you stan ;' at the
same time placing a bayonet at his breast in a manner that
told the officer that ' Potomac ' didn't pass in Missouri.
' What is the word, then ?' ' Buttermilk.' ' Well. then,
Buttermilk.' ' Dat is right ; now you pass mit yourself all
about your piziness.' There was then a general overhaul-
ing of the password ; and the difference between Potomac
and Buttermilk being understood, the joke became one of
the laughable incidents of the campaign.

————o————

Old Abe's Liquor for his Generals.

A ' committee,' just previous to the fall of Vicksburg,
solicitous for the morale of our armies, took it upon themselves to visit the President and urge the removal of Gen.
Grant. ' What for ?' said Mr. Lincoln. ' Why,' replied
the busybodies, ' he drinks too much whisky.' ' Ah !' rejoined Mr. Lincoln, ' can you inform me, gentlemen, where
General Grant procures his whisky ?' The ' committee '

confessed they could not. 'Because,' added Old Abe, with a merry twinkle in his eyes, 'If I can find out, I'll send every General in the field a barrel of it!' The delegation retired in reasonably good order.

————o————

Who voted for Abe, or how the Rebels treat a Quaker and a " Butternut."

The following incident occurred at Salem, Ind., during the raid of John Morgan. Some of his men proceeded out west of the town to burn the bridges and water-tank on the railroad. On the way out they captured a couple of persons living in the country, one of whom was a Quaker. The Quaker strongly objected to being made a prisoner. Secesh wanted to know if he was not strongly opposed to the South. 'Thee is right,' said the Quaker, ' I am.'

' Well, did you vote for Lincoln?'

'Thee is right; I did vote for Abraham.'

' Well, what are you?'

' Thee may naturally suppose that I am a Union man. Cannot thee let me go to my home?'

' Yes, yes; go and take care of the old woman,' said Secesh.

The other prisoner was taken along with them, but not relishing the summary manner in which the Quaker was disposed of, said, ' What do you let him go for? He is a black abolitionist. Now, look here, I voted for Breckinridge, and have always been opposed to this war. I am opposed to fighting the South, decidedly.'

'You are,' said Secesh; 'you are what they call around here, a Copperhead; ain't you?'

'Yes, yes,' said the Butternut, insinuatingly; 'that's what all my neighbors call me, and they know I ain't with them.'

'Come here, Dave!' halloed Secesh. 'There's a Butternut. Just come and look at him. Look here, old man, where do you live? We want that horse you have got to spare, and if you have got any greenbacks, just shell 'em out,'—and they took all he had.'

————o————

The President on Chase's Valentine.

Secretary Chase, of the Treasury Department, found upon a desk in his office what at first appeared to be a picture of an 'infernal machine,' looking very much like a goose, but which on closer examination proved to be a drawing of an ingenious invention for turning gold eagles into 'greenbacks,' with the Secretary himself operating it, and slowly feeding it with 'yaller boys' at one end, while the government currency came out at the other end, flying about like the leaves of autumn. While he was examining it, the President came in, as he daily does, for consultation. Mr. Chase handed him the drawing, and as the roguish eye of our Chief Magistrate recognised the likeness of the Secretary, he exclaimed—

'Capital joke, isn't it, Mr. Chase?'

'A joke,' said the irate financier, 'I'd give a thousand dollars to know who left it here.'

'Oh, no,' responded Mr. Lincoln, 'you would hardly do that.'

'Yes I would,' asserted the Secretary.

'Would you, though,' inquired the President, with that deliberate manner that characterizes him when he is really in earnest—' well, *which end would you pay from?*'

The answer is not ' recorded.'

————o————

Old Abo and the " Brigadiers."

The President has been perpetrating one of his pungent sayings about that luckless wight, Brigadier-General Stoughton, who was so unceremoniously picked up by guerillas. ' Pretty serious business, this, Mr. President,' said a visitor, ' to have a Brigadier-General captured at Fairfax Court House !' ' Oh, *that* doesn't trouble me, was the response, ' I can make a better Brigadier any time in five minutes ; but it *did* worry me to have all those horses taken. Why, sir, these horses cost us a hundred and twenty-five dollars a head !'

————o————

Mr. Lincoln and the " Mediums."

' There is a secret, known only to a few, in reference to the manner in which our armies are commanded,' says a New York writer. ' Mr. Lincoln has *mediums* in constant communication with the spirit world. Each military hero has a special medium. Not a battle has been fought, except under the direct command, not of McClellan, Scott,

McDowell, Pope, Burnside, Hooker, and modern generals, but they have acted merely as lieutenants for the master war-spirits of the other world !   All the generals in the other world were consulted by the spirits previous to Hooker's defeat, and the old adage proved true that ' too many cooks spoil the broth.'   Napoleon and Wellington, and Generals Washington and Jackson, were not at the council : Napoleon, because he did not understand Lincoln's English communications, and the Duke of Wellington, because of his contempt for them, or that anybody in supreme power should ask military advice.   Generals Washington and Jackson would not give advice, because, though they were extremely annoyed at the dissolution of the Union, yet, as such a miserable fact had occurred, their friendly feelings were enlisted with their descendants on the side of the South.   That Mr. Lincoln is guided altogether by spiritual advisers is now well known.'

————o————

Old Abe's Generosity.

While President Lincoln was confined to his house with the varioloid, some friends called to sympathise with him especially on the character of his disease.   ' Yes,' he said, ' it is a bad disease, but it has its advantages.   For the first time since I have been in office, 1 have something now to give to every person that calls.

Uncle Abe and the Pass to Richmond.

A gentleman called upon the President, and solicited a pass for Richmond. ' Well,' said the President, ' I would be very happy to oblige, if my passes were respected; but the fact is, sir, I have, within the past two years, given passes to two hundred and fifty thousand men to go to Richmond, and not one has got there yet.' The applicant quietly and respectfully withdrew on his tip-toes.

————o————

How Old Abe had never Read it.

' The Loyal League Convention, which was in secret session in Washington, brought a strong pressure to bear on the President for the removal of some obnoxious members of the cabinet on account of their supposed conservative views, and also for the appointment of a radical commander in Missouri, in place of Gen. Scofield. At an interview, a committee of the Leaguers indignantly asked the President whether he endorsed Mr. Blair's Rockville speech; to which he replied, that he 'had never read it.' The feelings of the excited radicals may be more easily imagined than described at this Lincolnian stroke, and they retired from the White House with no dim perception of the meaning of ' Abe's latest and best joke.'

Mr. Lincoln and the Counterfeit Bill.

'Some one was discussing the character of a copperhead clergyman, in the presence of Mr. Lincoln, a time-serving Washington clergyman. Says Mr. Lincoln to his visitor, 'I think you are rather hard upon Mr. Blank. He reminds me of a man in Illinois who was tried for passing a counterfeit bill. It was in evidence that before passing it he had taken it to the cashier of a bank and asked his opinion of the bill, and he received a very prompt reply that the bill was a counterfeit. His lawyer who had heard of the evidence to be brought against his client, asked him just before going into court, 'Did you take the bill to the cashier of the bank and ask him if it was good?' 'I did,' was the reply. 'Well--what was the reply of the cashier?' The rascal was in a corner, but he got out of it in this fashion: 'He said it was a pretty, tolerable, respectable sort of a bill.' Mr. Lincoln thought the clergyman was 'a pretty, tolerable, respectable sort of a clergyman.' We have a good many of that class in Washington, I fear, though, if anybody is going to make me prove this I'll back down at once, for in these times it is hard work to prove anything. If your neighbor is engaged in blockade running, you can't prove him a rebel; and if he should chance to be a noisy war politician, you can't prove that he has sympathies even against the government.'

A Whole Nager.

'At a negro celebration, an Irishman stood listening to Fred. Douglass, who was expatiating upon Government and freedom, and as the orator came to a period from the highest political heights, the Irishman said : ' Bedad, he spakes well for a nager.' ' Don't you know,' said one, 'that he isn't a negro ? he is only half negro.' ' Only a half nager, is he ? Well, if a half nager can talk in that style, I'm thinking a whole nager might beat the prophet Jeremiah.'

———o———

Old Abe and the Blasted Powder.

'A western correspondent writes : ' A visitor, congratulating Mr. Lincoln on the prospects of his re-election, was answered by that indefatigable story-teller with an anecdote of an Illinois farmer, who undertook to blast his own rocks. His first effort at producing an explosion proved a failure. He explained the cause by exclaiming, ' Pshaw, this powder has been shot before !'

———o———

' Hurrah for Abe Lincoln !' shouted a little patriot on Cedar street, the other day.

' Hurrah for the Devil ?' rejoined an indignant Southern sympathiser.

' All right,' said the juvenile ; ' you hurrah for your man, and I'll hurrah for mine.'

The President's Repartee,

A distinguished foreigner, dining at the White House, wished to congratulate President Lincoln on the self-possession of the hostess, and her apparent indifference to the peculiar vexations of her new position. Having an imperfect knowledge of our language, he expressed his idea by saying : ' Your Excellency's lady makes it very indifferent !' Observing the twinkle of the President's eye, he endeavored to correct his language, and immediately said with emphasis : ' Your Excellency's lady has a very indifferent face !'

————o————

" Salmon the Solemn," vs. Abraham the Jocular."

The solemn versus the jocular are brought into curious juxtaposition by the present state of affairs. The committee of ' the friends of Mr. Chase,' in their Ohio circular, call Mr. Lincoln ' our jocular President.' Against him they set up Mr. Chase, of whom a prominent Boston lawyer said some years ago, ' I don't like the Governor. He is too solemn—altogether too solemn.' More than a year ago, Mr. Lincoln said that he had just discovered that the initials of Salmon P. Chase mean shinplaster currency. Perhaps he will now say that they mean shinplaster candidate. An old Greek rhetorician advises to answer your adversary's sober arguments with ridicule, and his ridicule with sober argument.

Old Abe "glad of it."

A characteristic story of the President is narrated in a letter from Washington. When the telegram from Cumberland Gap reached Mr. Lincoln that 'firing was heard in the directon of Knoxville,' he remarked that he was 'glad of it.' Some person present, who had the perils of Burnside's position uppermost in his mind, could not see *why* Mr. Lincoln should be *glad* of it, and so expressed himself. 'Why, you see,' responded the President, 'it reminds me of Mistress Sallie Ward, a neighbor of mine, who had a very large family. Occasionally one of her numerous progeny would be heard crying in some out-of-the-way place, upon which Mrs. Sallie would exclaim, 'There's one of my children that isn't dead yet.'

———o———

Old Abe's "Affair of Honor."

Abraham Lincoln, at nineteen years of age, was six feet four in height, and so far exhibited the attributes of a ruler that he towered like Saul above his fellows. He was once, and once only, engaged in what is falsely termed 'an affair of honor.' A young lady of Springfield wrote a paragraph in a burlesque vein in a local newspaper, in which General Shields was good-humouredly ridiculed for his connexion with some public measure. The General was greatly incensed, and demanded of the editor the name of the offending party. The editor put him off with a request for twenty-four hours to consider the matter,

and shortly afterwards, meeting Lincoln, told him his per
plexity. 'Tell him I wrote it,' said Lincoln; and tell him
he did.   After a deal of diplomacy to get a retraction of
the offensive parts of the paragraph in question, Shields
sent a challenge, which Lincoln accepted, named broad-
swords as the weapons, and an unfrequented, well-wooded
island in the Mississippi as the place.   Old Abe was first
on the ground, and when Shields arrived he found his antagonist, his sword in one hand and a hatchet in the other,
with his coat off, clearing away the underbrush!   Before
the preliminary arrangements were completed, a Mr. Hardin, who somehow got wind of what was afloat, appeared
on the scene, called them both d—d fools, and by his arguments addressed to their common sense, and by his ridicule
of the figure that they, two well-grown, bearded men, were
making there, dissuaded them from fighting.

—————o—————

Mr. Lincoln's Disease.

President Lincoln has really had the small-pox, but is
able to have his joke regularly.   When the committee of
Congress waited on him to announce their readiness to
receive the message, the President was found in his private
office, clad in an old dressing-gown, and looking dilapidated
generally.   The chairman announced in a very formal
manner the object of the visit.   It seemed to please the
President mightily, and putting his hands deep in his
breeches pockets, and throwing a leg over an arm of his
chair, he replied: 'Well, if it is a matter of life and death

I can get it up to-day; but if it isn't, I'd rather wait till to-morrow, for the fact is the boys haven't got through copying it yet.' It was not a matter of life and death, and the message was not sent in till Wednesday. Mrs. Lincoln did not evidently think her husband was very sick, for she went to New York last week to do 'a little shopping.' While there she lost her purse, containing a large sum of money, in the street. It was found and returned to her by a young patent claim agent of this city, and Mrs. Lincoln was very profuse in her thanks and offers of assistance. The freedom of the White House was tendered to the young man, who, if he isn't too bashful, may consider his fortune made.

------o------

"The President was Reminded."

A gentleman was telling at the White House how a friend of his had been driven away from New Orleans as a Unionist, and how, on his expulsion, when he asked to see the writ by which he was expelled, the deputation which called on him told him that the government had made up their minds to do nothing illegal, and so they had issued no illegal writs, and simply mean, to make him go of his own free will. 'Well,' said Mr. Lincoln, 'that reminds me of a hotel-keeper down at St. Louis, who boasted that he never had a death in his hotel, for whenever a guest was dying in his house he carried him out to die in the street.'

President Lincoln on Grant's New Sword.

Just before Grant's arrival, Representative Washburne took to the White House a handsome sword, presented to General Grant by some admirers in Illinois, to show the President and Mrs. Lincoln. ' Yes,' said the President, ' it is very pretty. It will do for a Commander-in-Chief.' Old Abe then turned to a general officer then present and asked him if *he* had had any sword presentation lately. The reply was 'I have not.' 'Humph,' said Abe. ' that's a joke then that *you* haven't seen the *point* of yet.'

—— o ——

Abraham's Going to Pot.

' A deputation of gentlemen from New York waited upon Old Abe with the determination to impress his mind with the great injustice done their department of trade by the Committee on Taxation.

' Gentlemen,' said the President, ' why do you come to me? The committee will hear you and do you justice. I cannot interfere.'

' But,' urged the spokesman, ' if they are going to tax all the commodities of life,—'

' My friends,' responded the rail-splitter, ' if they tax all the necessaries, I'm afraid we must all go to pot.

Old Abe's " Mistakes."

' Old Abe being questioned one day in regard to some of his reputed ' mistakes' replied, ' That reminds me of a minister and a lawyer who were riding together; says the minister to the lawyer —

' Sir, do you ever make mistakes in pleading ?'

' I do,' says the lawyer.

' And what do you do with mistakes ?' inquired the minister.

' Why, sir, if large ones, I mend them; if small ones, I let them go,' said the lawyer. ' And pray, sir, continued he, ' do you ever make mistakes in preaching?'

' Yes, sir, I have.'

' And what do you do with mistakes ?' said the lawyer.

' Why, sir, I dispose of them in the same manner that you do. Not long since,' continued he, ' as I was preaching, I meant to observe that the devil was the father of *liars*, but made a mistake, and said the father of *lawyers*. The mistake was so small that I let it go.'

—— o ——

Speaking of the Time.

' When Mrs. Vallandigham left Dayton to join her husband, just before the election, she told her friends that she expected never to return until she did so as the wife of the Governor of Ohio.

Mr. Lincoln is said to have got off the following :—
' That reminds me of a pleasant little affair that occurred
out in Illinois.'

A gentleman was nominated for Supervisor. On leaving home on the morning of election, he said—

' Wife, to-night you shall sleep with the Supervisor of
this town.'

The election passed; and the confident gentleman was
defeated. The wife heard the news before her defeated
spouse returned home. She immediately dressed for going
out, and waited her husband's return, when she met him
at the door.

' Wife, where are you going at this time of night ?' he
exclaimed.

' Going ?' she replied, ' why, you told me this morning
that I should to-night sleep with the Supervisor of this
town, and as Mr. L. is elected instead of yourself, I was
going to his house.'

She didn't go out, and he acknowledged he was *sold*,
but pleasantly redeemed himself with a new Brussels
carpet.

————o————

Old Abe's Uncle.

' My deceased uncle,' says Old Abe, ' was the most polite
gentleman in the world. He was making a trip on the
Mississippi when the boat sank. He got his head above
the water for once, took off his hat, and said, ' Ladies and
gentlemen, will you please excuse me ?' and down he
went.'

Old Abe seeing the difficulty.

A very amusing scene was witnessed at the grand military dinner given at the Executive Mansion in honor of Lieutenant General Grant soon after his arrival here. After the guests had assembled and a brilliant array of well known military men appeared, in accordance with the President's invitation, to assist in the ceremonies of the evening, it was found, to the surprise of everybody that General Grant was not there. He had suddenly taken wings for the West. Everybody looked disappointed. Among the major generals present were. Halleck, Meade, Wool, McCook, Crittenden, Sickles, Hunter, Burnside, Blair, Doubleday, Ogilsby, Wallace and others. When it was announced that Grant was not coming the generals looked at the President and the President at the generals. Presently Mr. Lincoln said :—' Gentlemen, this is the play of Hamlet with Hamlet left out. We expected Grant here, but he couldn't stay.' The company had assembled, however, the curtain was raised, and the play must go on. But who would play the part of Hamlet? In plainer language, a lieutenant general was expected, but he would not be present. Old Abe, seeing the difficulty, said that if it was necessary to have a Hamlet he would call upon Major General Halleck at short notice, as the managers say, to fill that part. Halleck, who wore three stars on each shoulder, put on a most complacent appearance and ' kindly consented' to assume the *role* of the principal character And so the play went on, with Halleck as Hamlet.

One of Abe's Anecdotes.

Well,' said a gentleman to Old Abe, ' we had the nigger served up in every style last session.'

'Yes,' broke in the Executive, as his eyes twinkled. ' ending off with the *fire-cussee* style.'

' I hope,' resumed the gentleman, ' I hope we shall have something new now.'

'There was a man down in Maine,' said the President, 'who kep' a grocery store. and a lot of fellows used to loaf around that for their toddy.   Well, he only gave 'em New England rum, and they drinked a pretty considerable of it.   But after a while they began to get tired of that, and kep' asking for something New—something New; all the time.   Well, one night, when the whole crowd was around, the grocer, he sot out his glasses, and says he, 'I've got something New for you to drink, boys.' ' Honor bright,' says they. ' Honor bright ' says he; and with that he sot out a jug. ' Thar,' says he, ' that's something New ; it's *New*-England rum !' says he. ' Now,' remarked Abraham, shutting one eye, ' I guess we're a good deal like that crowd, and Congress is a good deal like that store-keeper !''

———o———

' What soldiers are these ?' asked Lincoln as a regiment marched by, ' Why, they belong to the new *levee* for the *Banks* of the Mississippi,' replied a ' mudsill' standing near.

How Old Abe Settled the Point.

The town is laughing at an amusing story of a recent interview between Mr. Lincoln and the president of the Baltimore and Ohio railroad. ' The draft has fallen with great severity upon the employes of our company,' said the R. R. President. ' Indeed !' responded the President of the U. S. ' If something is not done to relieve us, it is hard to foresee the consequences.' · Let them pay the commutation.' ' Impossible! the men can't stand such a tax.' ' They have a rich company at their back, and that's more than other people have.' ' They ought to be exempted, because they are necessary to the working of the road for the government.' ' That can't be.' ' Then I will stop the road.' ' If you do, I will take it up and carry it on.' The discussion is said to have dropped at this point, and the very worthy president is still working the road as successfully as ever.

————0————.

Old Abe was once canvassing for himself, for a local office, when he came to a blacksmith's shop.

' Sir,' said he to the blacksmith, ' will you vote for me ?'

' Mr. Lincoln,' said the son of Vulcan, ' I admire your head, but damn your heart!'

' Mr. Blacksmith,' returned Abe, ' I admire your candor, but damn your manners!'

The President's interview with a New Yorker.

A man from New York tells of an interview he had with the President. 'How are you,' said he. 'I saw your card, but did not see you. I was glad, however, that you carded me, and I was reminded of an anecdote of Mr. Whittlesey. When Mr. Cox, then a young man, first came here, Mr. Whittlesey said to him: 'Sir, have you carded the senators?' 'No sir; I thought I would curry favor first, and then comb them.' 'It is no joking matter, sir,' said Mr. Whittlesey, seriously. It is your duty to card the senators, sir; and it is customary I believe, to card the cabinet also, and you ought to do it, sir. But' he added, after a moment's thought, 'I think I am wrong; the cabinet may card you.'

————o————

Cool.--A gentleman visiting an hospital at Washington hearing an occupant of one of the beds laughing and talking about the President. He seemed to be in such good spirits that the gentleman remarked, 'You must be very slightly wounded?' 'Yes,' said the brave fellow, 'very slightly---I have only lost one leg.'

————o————

Old Abe's " Slap at Chicago.

Mr. Lincoln relates the following :

'Some years ago, when Chicago was in its infancy, a stranger took up his quarters at the principal hotel, and inscribed his name on the register as Mr. J——, of St.

Louis. For several days he remained there, engaged in transacting the business which had brought him to the place, and from his exceedingly plain dress, manners and general appearance, attracted but little attention.

Soon Mr. J——— was suddenly seized with illness, during which he was sadly neglected by his host; and the servants taking their tone from the master of the house, left him to shift for himself as best he could. Thus matters went on, till one morning he was past praying for; his papers were then examined, that the sad intelligence might be communicated to his friends; when to the surprise of all he was found to be one of the wealthiest men in the western country.

Arrangements were accordingly made for the funeral; but before the last rites were performed, the subject came to life again, having been the victim of catelepsy, instead of the grim ' King of Terror.' All were overjoyed at his fortunate escape from so dreadful a fate, and from that time were profuse in their expressions of solicitude, elicited, however, we judge, by ' documentary evidence,' rather than by any personal regard.

At length some one ventured to ask, how things appeared to him while in his trance, to which he thus replied:

' I thought I had come to the river of death, where I met an angel who handed me a jewel to serve as a pass to the other side. On giving this to the ferryman, I received from him another which carried me further another stage in my journey. Going on thus for several stages, receiving at the termination of each, a ticket for the succeeding one, I at last reached the gate of the Heavenly City. There I found St. Peter, who opened the door at my summons, pipe in mouth, seated by a small table, on which stood a goodly mug of steaming whiskey toddy.'

'Good morning, sir,' said he very politely.

'Good morning, St. Peter,' said I.

'Who are you, sir ?' said he, turning over the leaves of a huge ledger.

'My name is J——.'

'Very good, sir ; where do you live down below

'I lived at St. Louis, in the State of Missouri.'

'Very well, sir ; and where did you die ?'

'I died at Chicago, in Illinois.'

'Chicago ?' said he, shaking his head, 'there's no such place, sir.'

'I beg your pardon, St. Peter, but have you a map of the United States here ?'

'Yes, sir.'

'Allow me to look at it.'

'Certainly, sir.'

'With that he handed down a splendid atlas, and I pointed out Chicago on the map.

'All right, sir,' said he, after a moment's pause ; 'its there, sure enough, so walk in, sir ; but I'll be blest if you ain't the first man that has ever come here from that place !'

Thus ended Mr. J——'s account of his *transition* state ; and **no** more questions were asked. ''

Where Abe said it had gone.

When the Sherman expedition which captured Port Royal was fitting, there was great curiosity to learn where it had gone. A person visiting the Chief Magistrate at the White House importuned him to disclose the destination to him. ' Will you keep it entirely secret?' asked the President. ' Oh, yes, upon my honor.' ' Well,' said the President, ' I'll tell you.' Assuming an air of great mystery, and drawing the man close to him, he kept him a moment awaiting the revelation with an open mouth and great anxiety. ' Well,' said he in a loud whisper which was heard all over the room, ' the expedition has gone to—sea!'

—————o—————

A tall one by Old Abe.

That reminds us of the following story that has been told of Mr. Lincoln somewhere when a crowd called him out. He came out on the balcony with his wife, (who is somewhat below medium height,) and made the following ' brief remarks ': ' Here I am, and here is Mrs. Lincoln. That's the long and short of it.'

—————o— —

Abraham tells a Story.

Dr. Hovey, of Dansville, N. Y., thought he would call and see the President, and on arriving at the White House found him on horseback, ready for a start. Approaching him, he said :

' President Lincoln, I thought I would call and see you before leaving the city, and hear you tell a story.'

The President greeted him pleasantly, and asked where he was from.

'The reply was : ' From Western New York.'

' Well, that's a good enough country without stories,' replied the President, and off he rode.   That was the story.

———o———

Mr. Lincoln and the Georgetown Prophetess.

The President, like old King Saul when his term was about to expire, seems in a quandary concerning a further lease of office.   I lean that he has consulted again the ' prophetess ' of Georgetown, immortalized by his patronage.   She retired the other night to an inner chamber, and after raising and consulting more than a dozen of distinguished spirits from Hades, she returned to the reception-parlor where the Chief Magistrate awaited her, and declared that Gen. Grant would capture Richmond, and that Honest Old Abe would be next President.   She, however, as the report goes, told him to beware of Chase.

———o———

Sala.

It is reported that Old Abe let off a joke at George Augustus Sala.   It seems that eminent Bohemian, in a persevering search after information, learned to his astonishment that all our cavalrymen are furnished with a horse and two Colts each ; and his appetite duly whetted by this novel discovery, he made bold to inquire, in the presence of Old Abe, what branch of the service the Americans had experienced the most difficulty in becoming adepts?

'Engineering,' said the President, 'but unlike you Englishmen we experience little difficulty in building up that most essential thing an enduring magazine.'

The eminent George is said to have hemmed once or twice, in some doubt as to the exact application of this.

————o————

A Tight Squeeze.

President Lincoln says the prospect of his election for a second term reminds him of old Jake Tullwater who lived in Ill. Old Jake got a fever once, and he became delirious, and while in this state he fancied that the last day had come, and he was called to judge the world. With all the vagaries of insanity he gave both questions and answers himself, and only called up his acquaintances, the millers, when something like this followed:

'Shon Schmidt, come up here! Vat bees you in dis lower worlds?'

'Well, Lort, I bees a miller.'

'Well, Shon, did you ever take too much toll?'

'Oh, yes Lort, when the water was low, and the stones were dull, I did take too much toll.'

'Well, Shon,' old Jake would say, 'You must go to the left among the goats.'

So he called up all he knew and put them through the same course, till finally he came to himself:

'Shake Tullwater, come up here! Well, Shake, what bees you in this lower world ?'

'Well, Lord, I bees a miller.'

'And, Shake, didn't you ever take too much toll ?'

'Ah, yes, Lort, when the water was low, and the stones was dull, I did take too much toll.'

'Well, Shake—well Shake (scratching his head)—well Shake, what did you do mit dat toll.'

'Well, Lort, I gives him to de poor.'

'Ah! Shake—gave it to the poor, did you? Well Shake, you can go to the right among the sheep—hut it's a tam'd tight squeeze !'

—————o—————

At it with a Will.

The President and Secretary of State were closeted together, overwhelmed by the affairs of the nation.

'Seward, you look puzzled,' said Secretary Chase as he entered and found that able functionary half buried among papers, scratching his head and biting his pen.

'Never fear,' quoth Old Abe, laughing gaily and slapping the Secretary of State approvingly on the back. 'Where there's a Will there's a way !'

—————o—————

President Lincoln, in replying to the St. Louis delegation, which recently waited on him to urge the prosecution of the war on ultra Abolition principles, replied that 'he had more *pegs* than he had *holes* to put them in.' This answer is peculiarly appropriate, as the Abolitionists, since the commencement of hostilities, have been so much engaged in stealing as to render the war nothing but a game of cribbage.

Old Abe and the Bull-Frogs.

'A few days ago, Paine, a lawyer of some note in Cincinnati, paid a visit to the Presidential mansion, that he might return with his garments scented with loyal perfume to the Porkopolis Courts.

During the interview the President asked him what was the feeling of the people of Ohio in reference to the Presidential election. Mr Paine informed him that the great talk about Chase all amounted to nothing. At this announcement the President seemed well pleased and rubbing his hands, he exclaimed, 'That reminds me of a story. Some years ago two Irishmen landed in this country, and taking the way out into the interior after labor, came suddenly near a pond of water, and to their great horror they heard some bull-frogs singiug their usual song,— B-a-u-m!—B-a-u-m!—B-a-u-m! They listened and trembled, and feeling the necessity of bravery they clutched their shellalies and crept cautiously forward, straining their eyes in every direction to catch a glimpse of the enemy, but he was not to be found. At last a happy idea came to the most forward one and he sprang to his mate, and exclaimed, ' and sure, Jamie, it is my opinion it's nothing but a *noise.*'

————o————

Knowing too Much.

President Lincoln while entertaining a few select friends is said to have related the following anecdote of a man who knew too much.

During the administration of President Jackson, there
was a singular young gentleman employed in the public
Post Office at Washington.   His name was G.; he was
from Tennessee, the son of a widow, a neighbor of the
President, on which account the old hero had a kind
feeling for him, and always got out of his difficulties with
some of the higher officials, to whom his singular interfer-
ence was distasteful.

Among other things, it is said of him that while he was
employed in the General Post Office, on one occasion he
had to copy a letter to Major H., a high official, in answer
to an application made by an old gentleman in Virginia
or Pennsylvania for the establishment of a new post office.
The writer of the letter said the application could not be
granted, in consequence of the applicant's ' proximity' to
another office.   When the letter came into G.'s hands to
copy, being a great stickles for plainness, he altered
'proximity' to ' nearness to.'   Major H. observed it, and
asked G. why he altered his letter.

' Why,' replied G., because I don't think the man would
understand what you meant by proximity.'

' Well,' said Major H., ' try him ; put in the ' proximity,
again.'

In a few days a letter was received from the applicant,
in which he very indignantly said, ' that his father had
fought for liberty in the second war of independence, and
he should like to have the name of the scoundrel who
brought the charge of proximity or anything else wrong
against him.   There,' said G. ' did I not say so ?'

G. corried his improvements so far that Mr. Berry, the

Postmaster General said to him, ' I don't want you any longer, you know too much.'

Poor G. went out, but his old friend, the General got him another place. This time G's ideas underwent a change. He was one day very busy writing, when a stranger called in and asked him where the Patent Office was ?

' I don't know,' said C.

' Can you tell me where the Treasury Department is ?' said the stranger.

' No,' said G.

' Nor the President's house ?'

' No.'

The stranger finally asked him if he knew where the Capitol was.

' No,' replied G.

' Do you live in Washington, sir ?' said the stranger.

' Yes, sir,' said G.

' Good Lord ! and don't you know where the Patent Office, Treasury, President's House, and Capitol are ?'

' Stranger,' said G. ' I was turned out of the Postoffice for knowing too much. I don't mean to offend in that way again. I am paid for keeping this book. I believe I do know that much; but if you find me knowing anything more, you may take my head.'

' Good morning,' said the stranger.

Lincoln and the Curiosity Seeker.

In answer to a curiosity seeker who desired a permit to pass the lines to visit the field of Bull Run after the first battle, Mr. Lincoln made the following reply as his answer:

A man in Cortlandt county raised a porker of such unusual size that strangers went out of their way to see it. One of them the other day met the old gentleman and inquired about the animal. 'Wall, yes,' the old fellow said; 'he'd got such a critter, mi'ty big un; but he guessed he would have to charge him about a shillin' for lookin' at him.' The stranger looked at the old man for a minute or so; pulled out the desired coin, handed it to him and started to go off. 'Hold on,' said the other; 'don't you want to see the hog?' 'No,' said the stranger, 'I have seen as big a hog as I want to see.'

And you will find that fact the case with yourself, if you should happen to see a few *live* rebels there as well as dead ones.

————o————

Old Abe and the Copperhead.

A certain politician being rather loud in his denunciations of the administration in the president's hearing a short time since, he conveyed a very wholesome lesson in the following story, there was a Dutch farmer once who being just clad in the ermine of a justice of peace, had his first marriage in this way:

'Vell, you want to be marrit, do you?'

'Yes,' answered the man.

'Vell, do you lovish dis voman as goot as any voman you have ever seen?'

'Yes.'

Then to the woman:

'Vell, do you love this man so better as any man you have ever seen?'

She hesitated and he repeated:

'Vell, vell do you like him so vell as to be his wife?'

'Yes, yes,' she answered.

'Vell, dat ish all any reasonable man can expect; so you are marrit. I pronounce you man and wife.'

The man drew out his pocket-book and asked the justice what was to pay.

'Nothing at all, nothing at all, you are welcome to it if it will do you any goot.'

--------o--------

In speaking of certain odd doings in the Army, Old Abe said that reminded him of another story, as follows:

On one occasion, when a certain General's purse was getting low, he remarked that he would be obliged to draw on his banker for some money. 'How much do you want, father?' said the boy. 'I think I shall send for a couple of hundred,' replied the General. 'Why, father,' said his son very quietly, 'I can let you have that amount.' You can let me have it!' exclaimed the General in surprise; 'Where did you get so much money?' 'I won it at playing draw poker with your staff, sir!' replied the

hopeful youth. It is needless to say that the 9-40 train
next morning bore the 'gay young gambolier' toward his
home. Do you see the point.

————o————

Old Abe and the Woodcock.

The President one day dined at Richmond. When the
landlord produced his bill, he thought it very exorbitant, and asked his name,' ''Partridge! an't please you, replied the host. 'Partridge!' said he; 'it should be
woodcock, by the length of your bill.'

——o——

Old Abe and the Set Speech.

The President being recently importuned to deliver a
set speech for a *certain* specified purpose, said that the
request reminded him of an old story he once heard of a
couple of U. S. Senators.

It was on one of those memorable days when the Kan-
sas-Nebraska bill was being debated, Senator Seward
tapped Douglas on the shoulder, and whispered in his ear
that he had some ' Bourbon' in the Senator's private room
which was twenty years old, and upon it he desired to get
Douglas's judgment. The 'little giant' declined, stating
that he meant to speak in a few minutes, and wished his
brain unclouded by the fumes of liquor. At the conclu-
sion of his speech Douglas sank down exhausted in his
chair, hardly conscious of the congratulations of those who
flocked around him. At this juncture Seward seized one

orator's, arm, and bore him off to the Senatorial sanctum.

'Here's the Bourbon, Douglas,' said Seward ; 'try some —its sixty years old.'

'Seward,' remarked Douglas, 'I have made to-day the longest speech ever delivered ; history has no parallel for it.'

'How is that?' rejoined Seward, 'You spoke about two hours only !'

'Don't you recollect that a moment pefore I obtained the floor you invited me to partake of some Bourbon twenty years old, and now immediately after closing my remarks, you extend to me some of the same liquor, with the assertion that it is sixty years old ! a forty years speech was never delivered before.'

Seward acknowledged the 'corn,' and the two enemies (politically) smiled.'

———o———

Mr. Lincoln being found fault with for making another 'call' said that if the country required it, he would continue to do so until the matter stood as described by a Western Provost Marshal out West who says :

'I listened a short time since, to a butternut clad individual, who succeeded in making good his escape, expatiate most eloquently on the rigidness with which the conscription was enforced south of the Tennessee river. His response to a question propounded by a citizen ran somewhat in this wise : 'Do they conscript close over the river ?' 'Hell, stranger, I should think they did ! *They take every man who hasn't been dead more than two days!*' if this is correct the confederacy has at least a ghost of a chance left.'

And of another, a methodist minister in Kansas, living on a small salary, who was greatly troubled to get his quarterly instalment. He at last told the non-paying trustees that he must have his money, as he was suffering for the necessaries of life. 'Money!' replied the trustees, 'you preach for money?' We thought you preached for the good of souls!' 'Souls!' responded the reverend. 'I can't eat souls—and if I could, it would take a thousand such as yours to make a meal!' That soul is the point, sir, said the President.

———o———

Mr. Lincoln Telleth Another Story.

Judge Baldwin, of California, an old and highly respectable and sedate gentleman, called a few days since on Gen. Halleck, and presuming upon a familiar acquaintance in California a few years since, solicited a pass outside of our lines to see a brother in Virginia, not thinking that he would meet with a refusal, as both his brother and himself were good Union men. 'We have been deceived too often,' said General Halleck, 'and I regret I can't grant it.' Judge B. then went to Stanton and was very briefly disposed of with the same result. Finally he obtained an interview with Lincoln, and stated his case 'Have you applied to General Halleck?' inquired the President. 'And met with a flat refusal,' said Judge B. 'Then you must see Stanton,' continued the President. 'I have, and with the same result,' was the reply. 'Well, then,' said Old Abe, with a smile of good humor, 'I can do nothing ; for you must know *that I have very little influence with this Administration.*'

————o————

The Vice-President.

Vice-President Hamlin must get some new clothes. During a recent visit to Boston an acquaintance who appreciated the character of the man rather than the external evidences of position and power, passing him in the street met a jolly Jack in full naval costume. Thinking it might be gratifying announcement, our friend pointed to the Vice-President, saying :

'There, my boy, is Mr. Hamlin, the Vice-President.'

Jack looked doubtful and dubious for a moment, and then indignantly said :

'Tell that to the marines. Do you suppose that your Uncle Abraham would let the Vice-President loose in that sort of rig; see, he's got a cable tier kink in his hat, and he's pretty darned seedy all over. If he isn't one of Jeff Davis's guerrillas, he's in danger of being picked up for one, if he goes where Uncle Sam's men keep their weather eye open.'

————o————

President Lincoln Presented with a Pair of Socks.

At the Presidential reception on Saturday, Major French presented to the President a pair of woollen socks, knit

expressely for the President by Miss Addie Brockway, of
Newburyport, Mass.   On the bottom of each was knit the
secession flag; and near the top the glorious stars and
stripes of our Union, so that when worn by the President
he will always have the flag of the rebellion under hs feet.
These socks were sent by the maker to Mrs. Wm. B. Todd,
of this city, and at her request Major French presented
them with a few appropriate remarks.   They were most
pleasantly and graciously received by the President.

———o———

Lincoln's First and Last Night in New Orleans.

'The cholera was raging at the time I last visited New
Orleans 'Twas just dusk and everything seemed unusual
quiet.   I met but few people as I hurried on to the St.
Charles, which I found after repeated enquiries.   Everything had a neglected, deser . wo-begone look which
was rather home-sickening.   So I supped, called for a
room and went to bed but not to sleep, for the musquetoes,
oh! horrors, were as thick as bees in a hive; they bit, bit,
bit, till I felt as if every pore in my body was furnishing
supper to a horde of savages.   In vain I sloped and fought,
they were too much for me, I dressed myself, determined
to walk the streets till morning before I would suffer such
torment.   It was not very dark nor very light, just sufficient to discrn objects when your eyes became accustomed
to the darkness; I had barely emerged into the street when
I hit my foot against something and fell full length across
it on the walk; picking myself up I began to feel to see

what it was; just then a light appeared with two men bear
ing a coffin, which was placed on the one I had fallen over
my first impulse was to get back to my room, but the
knowledge of the infernal insects which infested it deter-
ed me, and I hastened on; I had not gone far when I fetch-
ed bolt upright. Well, this is queer, I thought, no more
coffins I hope—but the low tone of several men as they removed them into a cart that stood ready, convinced me as
well as my eyes which were getting used to the darkness.
I counted one, two, three, and up to fifteen; my heart sick-
ened, I turned, retraced my steps; warfare was better than
this, though my foes were legions.   Dark, shadowy forms
were flitting every few steps across the way bearing the
dead; no sound was heard i n the street, save the low rum-
ble of carts filled with victims to the dreadful scourge.
I found my room at last—how, I never knew; I laid down
and prayed for the morning light, but the musquitoes, as
if to make up for the lost time, redoubled their depredations.   An idea struck me, I would get under the bed and
perhaps elude them, I did and had peace for full five minutes
how I enjoyed it; but they found me, and I beat a retreat;
feeling about I discovered a fire-place and a wooden fire-
board partly before it.   I have it, and my heart gave one
leap of joy, I shook my fist at the humming torments, and
doubling myself up, crawled into the fire-place, bringing
the fire-board after me the best I could; I had air, and if it
did not smell very pure, why it was better than having
one's blood drawn away in the smallest possible fractions,
let alone the sensation after it; the stench grew stronger
and stronger.   No wonder, thought I, that people die here.
I began to grow curious and commenced feeling about me

cautiously first, then more daring, my hand went down into a vessel containing, not exactly cider and dough-nuts, but what might have passed for them if eyes only were used. I found some water and after washing over and over again that hand, I went below, enquired if any vessel was to leave that day, for it was already light and the inmates astir. They said yes, and with rapid strides I found my way to the levee where a steamer was ready to sail. Thank Heaven, I muttered, business must take care of itself, I'm off. The remembrance of that awful night will haunt me to the grave.'

————o————

Too Good to be Lost.

'Old Abe,' who presides at the National White House, is very fond of a good joke, and is in the habit of telling them, greatly to the amusement, and not unfrequently at the expense of his most particular friends. We have heard one lately, which, we think, will turn the tables upon the President. The conversation is said to have occurred between an old Illinois farmer and a member of Congress from Missouri, at Willard's Hotel, in Washington city.

Mr. R., the member, was in one of the sitting rooms of the hotel, quietly puffing his cigar and reading the New York 'Herald,' when he was approached by a rough, burly, middle-aged man, and the following dialogue is said to have occurred between them :

ILLINOIS FARMER. 'Sir, to make free, I understand you

are a member of Congress from the great State of Missouri.'

MR. R.   ⌒You are correctly informed, sir, I represent the —————— Congressional District, in that State.'

I. F.   'I am from Illinois, sir; am in Washington city, on no particular business—just looking round a little, to see how 'the cat jumps.'

MR. R.   'I am glad to know you, sir ; Illinois and Missouri ought to be good friends. and I shall be most happy to serve you in any way that I can.'

I. F.   'Well, sir, I don't want anything except to see this d——d infernal rebellion put down, it's nearly ruined us out West; I have already lost one son, and I would not be surprised if I lost them all before the war is over, for they are all in it, several of them with that brave fellow, John Logan.'

MR. R.   'Sir, you have my earnest sympathies, both in your desire to see the rebellion crushed, and in the severe loss you have met with in the death of your son.   I hope the Government will finally triumph in this wicked war, which has been forced upon it.'

I. F.   'Are you much acquainted in Illinois?   Do you know Mr. Browning? and if so what do you think of him ?'

MR. R.   'I know Mr. Browning very well, sir.   I think very highly of him.   He is a good man, sir, and one of the first statesmen of the country.'

I. F.   'Well, sir, are you acquainted with 'old Dick ?' he's been my representative in Congress for a long while.

MR. R.   'You allude, I suppose, to Col. Dick Richardson, of Quincy ?'

I. F.   'He's the b'hoy, sir ; what do you think of him ?'

MR. R.   'Col. R. is a patriotic and good man, a little too much steeped in Democracy.'

I. F.   'Never mind his Democracy, that will never hurt him half so much as the mean whiskey he drinks ; I tell you, Dick's a glorious fellow ; I like to hear him after that miraculous genius, Trumbull, who, I 'spose, wears as small a gizzard as any man that ever entered the Senate. After all though, my friend Stephen A. was the man, he could ' take the starch out of any of them,' and if he had lived, sir, I believe this infernal rebellion would have been over.'

MR. R.   ' Very likely, sir, ; Mr. Douglass was a noble man ; he would have exerted a vast influence, if he had lived, over the fate of our unhappy country.'

I. F.   ' Well, sir, do you know ' Old Abe?'

MR. R.   ' I have that honor.'

I. F.   'Well, I don't consider there is much honor about it, but I'd just like to know what you think of him.'

MR. R.   ' Well, sir, I am inclined to think well of the President : I believe he loves his country, sir.   He is surrounded by great difficulties, and is doing the best he can to surmount them.   He is frequently persuaded to do things which I think his better judgment does not approve, I believe he is honest, sir.'

I. F.   'Well, my friend, I see that 'Abe' has rather taken you in.   I know him a devilish sight better than most men.   I have known him 'like a book' for thirty-five years.   I knew him when he was a rail-splitter, and I tell you he never did an honest day's work at the business in his life. If he had 100 rails to hew he always got them from somebody else's pile! I knew him when he was a grocery keeper, and he always kept bad whiskey, cut a fellow's dram short, and charged two prices. With some folks Lincoln had the reputation of being very honest and not very smart ; but I tell you, sir, he's d——d smart and none too honest? (somewhat excited and the crowd gathering around). I tell you, sir, I know ' Abe' like a book, sir, and by the eternal, what I say is true?'

Mr. R. (Somewhat confused)—' Sir, I was just about taking a mint julep ; will you have the kindness to join me?'

I. F. ' If you are tired of talking, with all my heart, sir. Missouri and Illinois must stand together, sir. I tell you, by the shades of Old Hickory and Benton, they must work and fight for the old Union, Missouri and Illinois are the greatest States in the Union, sir. If they'll stand together, breast to breast, they can knock h—ll out of South Carolina and the whole South, and then, if need be, turn round and shovel New England into the ocean.'

Exeunt to the bar room.

————o————

Mrs. Old Abe.

(From the New York Mercury.)

Mrs. Lincoln is a short, stout, cheery, motherly little woman, of about forty years of age, more or less. Our artist has given us an excellent portrait of her pleasant but by no means handsome face, from a photograph taken

by one of our best operators.   Mrs. Lincoln was born in
Kentucky.   She might have been a native of Bourbon
County, for her maiden name was Todd ; but that portion
of the State was not thus honored.   At a comperatively
early age, after receiving a moderate educati᠁ ᠁ he left
her ' old Kentucky home' and removed to Il᠁ ᠁ s, where
she married Mr. Lincoln, then a young law, er of little
practice, who made up for his low standing at the bar by
standing over six feet high in his stockings.

It appears that Mrs. Lincoln was quite a village-belle
before her marriage, and had other suitors besides Honest
Old Abe.   One of them, a militia General, picked a quar-
rel with Mr. Lincoln about a satirical poem, which Mrs.
Lincoln had written and which Mr. Lincoln fathered.
The exasperated General sent a challenge to Mr. Lincoln,
which was at once accepted.   Mr. Lincoln was allowed
the choice of weapons, and chose cavalry-swords.   When
the General came to fight the duel, he was not a little
astonished at some of the arrangements.   Mr. Lincoln had
selected a field across which ran a high rail-fence.   The
terms of the combat were, that he should take one side of
the fence and the General the other ; that each should be
at liberty to keep as far away from the fence as he pleased,
but that neither should be permitted to climb over, crawl
through, or creep under the fence, upon any pretext whatever.   The General indignantly declined to take part in
such a combat, and Mr. Lincoln was declared the winner
of this novel tournament, and bore off his bride in triumph.
Mr. Lincoln has always been called a strict temperance-
man ; but it cannot be denied that, when he married he
took a Todd for life.

As her husband rose in the world, Mrs. Lincoln rose with him. He turned politician, went to the State Legislature, gained some eminence in the Illinois courts, and was finally elected to Congress. This progress was so gradual, however, that Mrs. Lincoln troubled herself very little about it. She was busy enough keeping house and tending to the babies, which arrived in not inconsiderable numbers. At first the only perceptible changes in her fortune were, that she hired 'help' to assist her in her housework, which she had previously done herself, and fitted up her residence in a more comfortable and tasteful style. Then she began to go into society, and into better society than the village of Springfield could afford. Judges and members of Congress, and sometimes United States Senators dropped in to see Old Abe, who had already been marked by shrewd observers as the coming man—or, as the Westerners expressed it, as · a good log to make something out of.' At last the great revolution came. Mr. Lincoln was nominated for the Presidency. Springfield became the political Mecca. Mrs. Lincoln was courted and flattered. Then Honest Old Abe was elected, and Mrs. Lincoln was the wife of the President of the United States. This elevation must have seemed to her magical. Censorious people have said that it almost deprived her of her senses. No wonder.

When President Lincoln made his grand tour through the country, on his way to Washington, Mrs. Lincoln accompanied him, and was, like him, ' the observed of all observers.' She kissed all the children at all the stations between Springfield and Washington, and accepted bouquets enough to fill the White House. Politicians and place-seekers fluttered about her in the cars, during the trip, in order to profit by her influence over Mr. Lincoln. Some few of them succeeded, and owe their offices to her intercessions upon their behalf. Those who saw the Presidential pair during this tour, describe them as an honest, simple, good-hearted, affectionate, innocent country-people, bewildered by the novelty of their surroundings, and quite at the mercy of the political sharpers who hovered around them like hawks. Upon the arrival of the special train at the Thirthieth-street depot in this city, the scene between Mr. and Mrs. Lincoln was quite touching. She took a brush and comb from her reticule, smoothed his hair, arranged his cravat, brushed some of the dust from his coat, and then stood looking at him with evident admiration. ' Am I all right now, mother ?' asked the President. Mrs. Lincoln's reply was a hearty kiss. Some of the spectators of this little episode—men who had not indulged in a bit of natural sentiment since childhood—rushed from the car, unable to restrain their laughter. But others, appreciating not only the republican simplicity but also the conjugal tenderness of the scene, were quite otherwise affected by it.

Mr. Lincoln, it will be remembered, ran away from the Presidential party at Harrisburg, and entered Washington at night, disguised in a Scotch cap and a long military cloak. Mrs. Lincoln passed through Baltimore the next day, and was neither assassinated, insulted, nor annoyed. The evening after her arrival in Washington, she gave a reception at Willard's Hotel. The parlors were crowded with elegantly-dressed ladies and gentlemen, the belles and beaux of the capital. By and by, President Lincoln entered, feeling and looking very awkward in his new suit of clothes, and leading Mrs. Lincoln by the hand. 'Ladies and gentleman,' said he, after an embarrassing pause, 'here you see the long and the short of the Presidency '— indicating first himself and then his wife. The belles bowed and buried thire faces in their handkerchiefs to conceal their smiles. The beaux dashed frantically out into the lobbies, aching with irrepressible mirth. This was Mrs. Lincoln's introduction to Washington society. A relative named Mrs. Grimsby, was sent for to teach the President's wife etiquette, and for a while no parties were given at the White House. Then came the famous ball, which so exercised the Radical Abolition and religious press. We have not space to dwell upon this topic ; nor upon the scandal about Mrs. Lincoln's rebel relatives ; nor upon the charges that Mrs. Lincoln revealed the military secrets of the Administration ; nor upon the insinuations that this General was promoted and that disgraced, this official appointed and that removed, because of Mrs. Lincolns whims. These stories — once thought of sufficient importance to be published in the daily papers and investigated by a Committee of Congress—were long since exploded, and must be familiar with all our readers, who will join with us in despising those who originated such base slanders.

Mrs. Lincoln has traveled over the North quite extensively during the past four years, and is always attended by her little suite of officers and place-holders. Three years ago, she held her Republican Court at Long Branch during the summer. An amusing incident occurred at a ball given there in her honor. She did not dance, but stood in front of an arm-chair on one side of the hall, like a queen before her throne. The rest of the company were dancing when supper was announced, and they hurried tumultuously out of the room, forgetting all about Mrs. Lincoln, and leaving her and her immediate attendants to take care of themselves. From this incident two deductions may be made: first, the company were exceedingly ill-bred ; and, second, that Mrs. Lincoln does not inspire people with a sense of her personal dignity and importance. Both deductions are correct. Mrs. Lincoln is just as we have described her—a plain, good-natured, chatty, sociable amiable, agreeable, house-wifely, little woman, never designed to shine in the drawing-room, and ignorant of many of the conventionalities of fashionable life, but not the less admirable for all that. She likes fine dresses and fine company, and flattery and homage, as what other ladies do not? If, as some of her feminine critics remark, her position as wife of the President has quite turned her head, this can readily be pardoned, since it is enough to have turned many a wiser one. Before these feminines criticise Mrs. Lincoln too severely, they should consider how they would feel if they were in her place—as they may be some fine day, if their husbands are fortunate enough. Queen Victoria, the best of queens, is a homely, dumpy, German woman, who would not look out of place in a lager-bier saloon, so far as mere personal appearance goes. And, on the other hand, there have been ladies in high position who were celebrated for beauty of face and figure, elegance of manners and perfection in all the fashionable arts, and whose conduct has yet disgraced themselves, their sex, and their rank. This can never be truly said of Mrs. Abraham Lincoln.